Blackula the Vampire!

Walter Foster

Published by The New Star Press, 2023.

This is a work of fiction. Similarities to real people, places, or events are entirely coincidental.

BLACKULA THE VAMPIRE!

First edition. February 2, 2023.

Copyright © 2023 Walter Foster.

ISBN: 979-8215766323

Written by Walter Foster.

Also by Walter Foster

Tour of Atlantis
The House on the Edge of Homerville
Blackula the Vampire!
The Invisible Man
Blackenstein
Diamonds on Mars!
Fragments: Abort Martian Landing
Madam Black Soothsayer - Fortune Teller

to Cindy

BLACKULA
THE VAMPIRE !
BY

Walt Foster

B*LACKULA*
The Vampire !

Chapter

One

GEORGIA, U.S.A.
OCTOBER, 2017

It was the woman he wanted! And he wanted her at all cost!

---

*H*e *was* tall; over six feet. He was groomed to the last detail, and sported a thick black mustache. He had a powerful physique. He had a deep, rich baritone voice. He always bowed courteously. He bowed to many of those he would meet. He bowed a lot.

But wait: he was not at all as he seemed to be, for *he was Blackula a product of the night!;* And it was the *woman* he wanted; the one beautiful woman; a woman from his past. But she was NOT the same woman; she only looked like her in face and features. But still, he wanted her at ALL cost!!!

H*e was* obviously from a foreign country by the way he was dressed; a traditional Dashiki robe, native to his land. He looked to be about forty or so years, his dark hair, widows peak and mustache making him seem all the more distinquished but *disquised* the horror he held within.

It had been a long journey from Monrovia, East Africa where he was born to the U.S. He flew commercial just like anyone else.

He spoke to no one on the plane.

I*t was* not at all easy for him getting into the States where he would start his prowl; his odd search for the woman he once knew, the woman he once knew in the States; the beautiful woman he wanted to make like him; foul, evil; a *thing* of the night.

Soon, his night flight was in Atlanta, Georgia and Hartsfield International Airport. He purposefully arrived at 7:00 p.m. in the darkness, daring not to come out into the daylight.

Blackula was then ready to launch his diabolical plan; to make the woman his!

He *noticed* that not much had changed in the ten decades he had visited the country, the U.S. The Cabbie **took him on a half hour ride to a rural twenty five acre farm outside of the city called** *Grant Plantation.* **It was a rather quaint looking typical farm with a barn, chickens, and of course, a large two story brick house. It was a cozy setting; remote; isolated and far away from people;** *a perfect hideaway to execute his plans!*

U*pon arrival,* the two men got out of the car. The **tall Liberian opened his wallet and handed the cabbie** *funny money;* **money the cabbie did not recognize.**

"I can't take that," the cabbie said, his eyes wide.

"Oh, forgive me," the Liberian said, in his thick African accent. It was African money.

The annoyed cab driver went no further into it and recognized that it was an honest mistake. The man checked into another compartment of his wallet and found *American* currency and provided it to the driver; almost two hundred dollars.

The driver looked at the tall Liberian man with new respect.

"Thanks!" the cab driver said, taking the money.

He offered the Liberian man his change.

"Keep it," the mysterious man said, lowly.

The mysterious man opened the back door of the cab and took out his luggage, a lone suitcase.

He closed the door. The cabbie climbed into his cab, waved his hand and drove away, leaving the man standing alone several feet from the front door.

A man ran out of the house extending his hand to the man.

"Mister Okimbi! Professor Okimbi! How good it is to meet you, Sir! How good it is to see you!" the man said.

The two men shook hands friendlily.

"I am Professor Okambe Okimbi of Liberia," the man said, bowing deeply.

"And I'm Horace Grant, owner and proprieter of this farm, at your service," he said, clicking his heels together.

"It is a pleasure to finally meet you, Mister Grant," the man said, bowing. "I appreciate your thought and consideration."

"Don't mention it. I'm tickled you're here! I hope this place is suitable?" Mr. Grant asked, still with much enthusiasm.

The tall man looked around the farm.

"This place is charming, Sir," he said.

He looked back at the man. "I believe our written agreement was for a week? Of course, you will be amply compensated."

"Oh, don't worry about that now, Professor. Just having you here is almost payment enough," Mr. Grant said.

Mr. Grant looked at the tall man's luggage. "You travel light."

"I bring only the things I need for my weeks stay and my purpose: that is to say, my research," he said, in his deep voice.

"Yes. I suppose you're research is constantly on your mind. Your letters, credentials and documents stated that you were a university professor and writer and the papers you sent to me would be part of a book: an anthology about different parts of the world. I'm glad to be a part of that. You said you requested lounging while you completed this book on human culture. Needless to say, I found this very fascinating and I was thrilled you even considered me. Of course, I immediately researched you. Your credentials turned out to be exquisite and you are a well respected man that many in your country vouch for," Mr. Grant said.

"My university and colleagues are all too kind," the Liberian man said.

"I read the thesis paper you sent to me on African culture, Professor. I see you have visited many nations on that continent. Obviously you have learned a lot from the people there. Your research is in depth, *involving,* and you understand human nature and how basically we all pretty much the same. I thought it was brilliant! You have to be one of the foremost experts in human culture!" Mr. Grant said.

"Enough, Sir. You are embarrasing me, but I thank you," the man said, bowing again.

"Well, we've arranged things so you may avail yourself to your private library and it's many books. The library is in the exact room where you will be staying. I think you will find it most convenient. Please come in," Mr. Grant said.

Mr. Grant extended his hands backwards towards the front door. The man picked up his luggage and the two men entered the house.

Mr. Grant turned towards him. "I want you to meet my housekeeper, Flora. I've told her all about you. And she's very eager to meet you."

The man sat his luggage onto the floor. Mr. Grant led him past the living room and into the kitchen.

They saw a slender Black woman of about fifty years old cooking on the stove.

Mr. Grant looked at her. "Flora, stop what you are doing!"

She stopped fussing over her pots and pans.

Mr. Grant extended his arms backwards to the man. "I'd like for you to meet Mister, or rather, Professor Okambe Okimbi of Monrovia, Liberia. He's here, finally. As I said: he's a professor of the university there. So ask him good questions. And as we discussed, he'll be staying here for a week to study our Western culture to include it in his upcoming book. He wants to see how we eat; how we dance; how we act and so forth. So be on your best behavior," Mr. Grant said.

Flora smiled at the man.

"Pleased to meet you, Mr. Okimbi," she said, extending her hand to him.

They shook hands friendlily.

"Pleased to meet you, Miss Flora," he said, bowing, in his deep voice. "I've heard so much about you."

"And I've heard a lot about you," she said.

". . . All good, I hope?" he asked.

"All good," she answered.

Mr. Grant leaned over the pots on the stove.

"Ummmmm, uh!"

He looked at Flora. "I've bragged on your cooking to him. I hope you will serve up a few good dishes so we will get a good report."

"Mr. Grant, I haven't failed you yet," she said.

"I can safely say, you haven't," Mr. Grant said.

He looked at the two of them. "I'm only kidding Flora. She has been with me for fifteen years. She moved in here fifteen years ago when I was a lonely man and she hasn't left. I can't get rid of her. I guess at the time, we both needed each other. I'm glad the two of you are hitting it off."

Flora looked at the tall man.

"I hope you enjoy your stay, Mr. Okimbi," she said.

"I am enjoying it already, Mam," he said.

"Thank you. Dinner is at seven, Sir. And I hope it is as Mr. Grant would prefer: *to your liking,*" she said.

"Thank you. I am certain it will be, Miss Flora," he said, but in an unsmiling way.

Mr. Grant looked at the wall clock across the way in the living room.

"Well," he continued. "I see that it's five o'clock. Now that the introductions are out of the way, I'm sure you'd like to know where your sleeping quarters are located? Just take the stairs and it will be the first door to the right. I'm sure you'd like to freshen up before dinner?"

There was a staircase after the kitchen area and between the living room that led up to the second floor.

Mr. Okimbi bowed.

He went to where he had dropped his luggage near the front door, picked it up and headed for the stairs. Before he reached the top step Mr. Grant yelled up to him. "And don't forget to avail yourself to the many, many books and tapes we've placed in the makeshift library in your room. It has a desk and chair, a place for you to sleep; everything you will need for your research. You'll figure it out. Help yourself. My room is the connecting room to yours."

The Liberian man bowed.

"Many thanks," he said, looking back to them but again without a smile on this face.

He came to his room almost immediately to the right at the top of the staircase. He recognized Mr. Grants connecting room just to the right of his own.

Inside the room, the man saw hundreds upon hundreds of volumes of books; those of reference; dictionaries; books on foreign languages and cultures that had been provided for him.

And away from the books he noticed an open closet with many hangers, and a place for him to sleep.

He sat his suitcase on the floor.

His vampiric teeth began to show.

With brute strength, he ripped an entire section of books from it's shelves and they dropped to the floor.

"Thesis papers: BAH! Keep your hospitality! What do I need this for?" he asked himself.

His eyes were red. From where he stood he looked in the assumed direction where the woman lived: His voice became more gentle: "I am here, Marina. At long last I have found you again. You were mine once, Marina. Then we came apart. I was here once, in these America's: it's where we met, many decades ago. You are still beautiful. I saw a photo of you: a picture. And you will be mine again! And this time, no one is going to stand in my way!"

After a few seconds his teeth became normal again. Much calmer, he returned to his luggage and began to unpack.

Chapter

Two

It was soon seven o'clock, dinner time.

Flora served chicken and mashed potatoes in the dining room which was located between the kitchen and the living room.

Wine was also in their glasses.

Mr. Okimbi looked *normal*: as normal as could be for a man being what he was. The two men feasted on dinner and sipped their wine.

Flora approached the man at the table.

"More potatoes, Sir?" she asked him.

She had a bowl of hot mashed potatoes in her hand.

"You're feeding me too much," the man said, courteously. "But I will try some more."

She scooped a couple of spoonfuls into his plate. With a fork, she placed more chicken there.

The man looked at Mr. Grant. "You are right, she is an excellent cook."

"And a great housekeeper to," Mr. Grant said, while eating.

She went back into the kitchen and began to wash dishes. She looked back into the dining room at the man.

"So you're writing a book, Mr. Okimbi? What exactly is going to be in it?" she asked, curiously.

"Oh, nothing much. It concerns people: I've already traveled to Asia; Japan and the Philippines to collect data and live among them. Mr. Grant knows of my journey to different parts of Africa. I thought I'd come to America to write about the west, and compare my notes," he answered.

"Sounds interesting," she said, still doing her chores.

"Yes," the man said. "Ultimately, I am going to take my results back to my students in my classes. You will be surprised how interested they are in how other people live."

"Probably, there is not much difference," she said.

"Probably not," he agreed, taking a bite from off of his plate. "But the curiosity of one culture to another is there."

"Are you going to grade us, professor?" she asked, stopping for a moment.

"Oh, no. The book is strictly for informational purposes; not to put people into any kind of a *category*," he said.

"Excellent. Am *I* going to be in this book, Sir?" she asked.

The vampire chuckled.

"I would not be surprised, Miss Flora. I would not be surprised," he answered, staring directly at her.

He sipped graciously on his glass of wine.

She paused.

She looked dazed.

"That would be pretty good. . ." she laughed. ". . . Simple country girl finds her way into famous thesis paper and anthology book!"

"After a meal like this, it is well deserved," he said, finishing his meal.

He took a sip of his wine.

Mr. Grant was finishing his meal also. He had remained mostly silent.

He wiped his mouth with his napkin and looked at the two of them.

"Well, this can go on all night!"

He looked at Professor Okimbi. "Sir, what do you say we adjourn into the living room for a few cigars and a little more of these cocktails?"

"I would enjoy it very much," he said, in his deep African baritone.

"Great! Flora? Would you bring that fifty year old bottle of Burgundy in the pantry that I've been saving for a special occasion? We'll sample a drop or two of that before retiring," Mr. Grant said.

He stood up and went into the living room. Professor Okimbi followed him.

They sat on the couch.

Mr. Grant continued. "Professor, you and I are going to talk some more. After reading some of the papers you sent me, I'm convinced that you're both brilliant and *modest*. For instance, why do the Japanese people admire age?"

"It is their culture. In the west you admire youth and beauty. In the east they admire age and wisdom," the vampire said.

"Isn't that amazing? What else can you tell me, Sir, about the different way we live? I just want to pick your brain!" Mr. Grant exclaimed.

From the kitchen, Flora brought in two cocktail glasses, a bottle of Burgundy and cigars on a tray. The two men smoked, drank and laughed their way into the wee hours of the morning.

Then, Professor Okimbi abruptly excused himself. He began to seem uneasy. Restless. Listless! He went upstairs to his second floor room.

Flora opened her door to the left side of the staircase, opposite the right side where Professor Okimbi's room was located.

She was in her robe and had curlers in her hair. She saw Mr. Grant sitting silently and alone in the living room, finishing his cigar and drink. She started downstairs towards the living room. He looked in back of her and saw her before she had even reached the bottom step. "I thought I heard a noise. What are you doing up so late?"

"Is he gone?" she asked, looking here and there, her eyes wide.

"Who? Mr. Okimbi?"

"Yes."

He took another puff on his cigar.

". . . Said he was tired. He went upstairs to his room," Mr. Grant said.

"Good. I'm glad he left."

"Oh?"

"Yeah."

"What do you think of him? He's a very brilliant man, isn't he?" Mr. Grant asked.

"He gives me the *creeps!*" Flora said, abruptly.

Mr. Grant took the cigar out of his mouth.

". . . What?" he asked.

"I don't know, Sir. There's *something* about that man that ain't quite right; something I noticed from the moment he walked through that door. He looks at you: and it's like he's looking right through you. And when we shook hands; it was like shaking hands with an ice cube," she said, rubbing the chill off of her upper arms.

"Must be your imagination. I hadn't noticed things like that," Mr. Grant said.

"Well I have. Notice the way he shifts from side to side and turns away when you look at him directly. And he paced the room and looked outside in the dark yard at *nothing* in the middle of our conversation with him? Did you see that? What's the matter with him? Is he antisocial? Is he a creep or what?!" she asked, looking at Mr. Grant with all sincerity.

"Oh, I'm sure it's nothing," Mr. Grant said. "He drank my wine and smoked my cigars just like anybody, didn't he? No, he's just an average guy who's done very well for himself. Sometimes these men so brilliant have little idiocicrencies about themselves. We have to work around them."

"Poo. Work around. Just watch your back," she said. "Or do you want me to do that for you?"

"Go on to bed. Hurry, now. I'll see you at breakfast. I'm sure by that time you'll have forgotten this notion," Mr. Grant said.

"Thank you, Sir. I hope so. I don't like going around feeling the way I do about that man or any of your guests. I'll see you in the morning," she said.

Chapter

Three

LATER THAT SAME NIGHT

Flora was right.

The man took a walk in the wee hours of the morning, nearly two o' clock. After hearing a noise, she cracked open her door and saw him. She studied his slow, creepy gait down the stairs and out into the front yard.

She followed him and peeped out the front door that was barely open. He stood alone in the dark front yard. It looked as if he was howling at the moon!

He was saying something: *'Marina... Marina... Where are you, my Marina?'*

Flora looked puzzled.

'Who was this Marina?' she thought.

She forgot the entire question as his face turned a greenish color! With wide eyes she put her hand on her chest and backed away from the door in horror.

Then, and without warning, he returned to his original skin tone; a dark Black.

After several minutes she couldn't stand it any longer. She ran up the stairs to her room and slammed the door shut behind her!

Then there was Ann Thomas herself. She was young, 30, pretty, petite, African American, down to Earth and very smart. She was an Atlanta attorney, a partner in a prestigious law firm, unaware of what was going on around her.

For four years she and her husband, Doctor Stanley Thomas, had lived quietly next to Mr. Grant. Her husband was a well known physician in the Atlanta area, and they had gotten to know their neighbor, the widower Grant, very well.

She had no idea of the mechanizations occuring behind her back. She had no idea that she was being stalked!

Meanwhile, Okimbi, the vampire had reentered the house and up to his bed, his face had returned to normal, his greeness had turned to Black; his prominent teeth, normal again. He had been up half the night with cigars and wine and the night was nearly through. For the moment he would bide his time and not make himself known. It was nearly morning.

He had to sleep all day.

At breakfast he sat at the table (the dinning room table) with Mr. Grant. It wasn't quite seven o'clock in the morning and it was still dark outside a fact that did not go

unnoticed by Mr. Okimbi (the vampire).

"Nice morning," he said, rather lowly to the others.

Flora served eggs, toast, grits and bacon and the vampire ate like any other animal. She sat juice in front of him but he didn't bother to thank her. His mind was still on the woman he had come to take and he seemed to ignore everyone else as he enjoyed his toast and eggs.

Mr. Grant stared across the table at him.

He noticed how he seemed to be enjoying the eggs Flora had prepared.

"Those eggs are great, aren't they Mr. Okimbi?" he asked.

"Yes. They are most delicious," he said.

"Did you sleep okay, Mr. Okimbi?" Mr. Grant asked, going back to his eating.

"Yes. Thank you," he responded, taking a sip of his juice.

Mr. Okimbi stopped eating. "New atmosphere; new bed. It takes some getting used to, I suppose; but overall, very nice."

"I heard you walking around last night?" Mr. Grant asked. "Since we have connecting rooms it's hard not to hear."

"I needed a glass of milk to help me to rest," the African said.

"Well, like I said, you're welcome to anything around here. You almost bumped right into Flora. She's an early bird, you know, to make breakfast? You can set your watch by her," Mr. Grant said.

The man resumed his meal.

"I see. And you did a wonderful job, Miss Flora. I will go back to my country and tell my people of the wonderful cook I have encountered," he said.

The man finished his breakfast. He noticed that the dawn light was beginning to shine through the kitchen window. He stood up abruptly and hurriedly closed the curtains, cutting off the light.

Both Mr. Grant and Flora looked at him stunned.

He looked first at Flora and then at Mr. Grant. "I must apologize for my abruptness. The *glare* was beginning to hurt my eyes."

He wiped his mouth gracefully with his napkin.

He bowed gracefully. "Thank you, Mam, thank you, Sir, for that enjoyable breakfast. However, if you both will excuse me, I must get to my work. How do you American's say it: I am a. . . *'workaholic?'*"

"Lunch will be at noon," Flora said, still looking at him with wide eyes.

"That will not be necessary. I will be too busy," he said with firmness. Then he added more quietly: "However, I will be glad to join you both for dinner, if I may?"

"Delighted, to have you, Mr. Okimbi. I have to go off a bit to deliver some fruit to the market, but I'll be back by then. It'll be at the usual hour of seven," Mr. Grant said.

Mr. Okimbi bowed gracefully again and left the kitchen without saying another word. He walked up the staircase and entered his room to the right and closed the door behind him.

⸺ ⟨◦⟩ ⸺

U*pon entering* the room the man put his forehead up against the wall and slammed his fist into it. He threw things around the room. He thought he was so close.

⸺ ⟨◦⟩ ⸺

I*n his* stiff-like manner he sat at his desk Mr. Grant had provided for him. From it's top drawer, in the mist of hundreds of books, he pulled from it: the newspaper photograph of Ann Thomas that he had brought with him from Liberia. More and more, to him, she was beginning to look like Marina, his former love.

A gentleness came across his face; *a gentleness.* He looked at the photo with a great deal of happiness.

"Soon, you will be mine, MARINA, my love. At long last, we can be together! I have journeyed many thousands of miles and across one hundred and fifty years to make you mine again. Marina! Why did you leave me? We had so much together? Why?"

He hugged the photograph. He stopped.

He put the photo back into the top drawer of the desk. He turned to those at the table below. His infamous, dog-like teeth had started to show. He threw another tantrum by throwing things around the room again. "Mortals!"

He closed the top drawer. *His teeth looked normal again.* Then, awake, he roamed all night, and prepared himself not to do any work but to sleep all day.

Chapter

Four

LATER THAT SAME EVENING

Mr. Grant knocked on his door.

"Mr. Okimbi, it's seven o'clock. It's dinner time," he said.

"I shall be right down," the man said, through the door.

He dressed in his traditional Dashiki robe and made his way downstairs. He seemed more upbeat than earlier in the morning. It was dark outside and he had a whole night ahead of him. He sat in the dining room across from Mr. Grant. Mr. Grant was a little startled. He had never seen that particular robe before.

He looked at the man.

"Mr. Okimbi, you sure know how to dress for dinner. What did you say you called that outfit?" he asked.

"A Dashiki, my friend: traditional African dress," Mr. Okimbi answered.

"Very nice," Mr. Grant said.

He turned and looked at Flora who was fussing over pots and pans in the kitchen. "Doesn't he look nice, Flora?"

"You look nice, Mr. Okimbi; good enough to eat!" she yelled from the kitchen.

"Thank you," Mr. Okimbi yelled back. "I am sure you have seen these."

Flora came over with a pot in her hand.

"Yes, in books and magazines; never up close," she said.

"Well, there is a first time for everything," he said.

Mr. Grant seemed amused.

"Flora doesn't get out much. But her cooking makes up for everything. It's all she can do to take care of me. She's prepared chicken and dumpling tonight," Mr. Grant said.

He looked at Flora. "Give him some, Flora."

She put a generous helping on his plate.

"Hope you enjoy, Sir," she said.

"I am sure I will, Miss Flora," he said.

He began his meal.

Flora served Mr. Grant also.

Mr. Grant looked across the table at Mr. Okimbi.

"What did you do all day, Sir?" Mr. Grant asked.

"I continued to work on my thesis, of course; what I have seen since my arrival here. And I. . . *slept* on many ideas," he said.

"Excellent; make any progress?"

"Some. I think the thesis will be one of the chapters in my book. The room is somewhat confining. But your many books are very interesting and supportive. I suppose one must, in this instance, be concessive," Mr. Okimbi answered, in an upbeat fashion.

"Yes, I guess the room is rather small. You have to make adjustments," Mr. Grant said.

Mr. Grant snapped his fingers. "Say! I have an idea! You came here to size up our people, the boring Westerners, right? You didn't come here to just stare into a bunch of books all day, correct? I'm going over to the Thomas', Stan and Ann after breakfast tomorrow. They're married. They are a *model* couple; model citizens. She's a lawyer and he's a doctor. They know you were coming. I told them. I told them all about you and what you were doing here, and I let them read one of your thesis papers you sent me on other cultures.

Now is as good a time for you to meet them as any. They'll be tickled pink to meet you! I serve some of the supermarkets around here; bringing them fruit from my orchard. I also serve some of the locals; including them. I'm bringing them fruit in the morning and I want you to come along. I know they'll enjoy meeting you and I think you'll enjoy meeting them! You may even get some feedback on some of our behavior here in the west! What do you say, Mr. Okimbi? Want to come?"

It was just what Mr. Okimbi had come for.

"Sounds interesting," he said.

"Then it's settled! We'll start out first thing after breakfast in the morning," Mr. Grant said.

"Excellent. I would enjoy making friends of your people," Mr. Okimbi said.

The vampire stretched. He stood up from the table. "I must give my apologies but it has been a long day. I think I shall retire to my room; perhaps some study. I will see you in the morning."

"Very good, Mr. Okimbi," Mr. Grant said.

The vampire looked at Flora.

"And to you, Miss Flora, it was a very nice dinner; my compliments," he said, bowing.

He bowed to Mr. Grant and walked away. He headed slowly up the staircase and disappeared into his room. Mr. Grant remained at the dining room table sipping his coffee.

Flora walked to the back of him.

"I said it before and I'll say it again: *there is something odd about that man,*" she said.

"Odd? Flora, you're not going to start that again?"

"Mr. Grant, it's like he's *hiding* something. I can see it in his bloodshot eyes," she said.

"Hiding what? The man has one suitcase and a couple of long shirts. AND one of the most impeccable records I have ever seen. What could he be hiding?" Mr. Grant asked.

"I don't know," she said.

Flora walked past him and looked up at his room. "But the day he walked in here I sensed it. And the day he leaves will be a good day! And did you notice how fast he went up to his room; like he had somewhere to go? And where could he be going, except to sleep?"

He looked at her.

"Again, I think you're just imagining things. He hasn't adopted to our ways yet; the way we do things here. Give him a chance. That's why I want him to get out and meet people like the Thomas' so he can get a better idea of how we are, of WHO we are. And remember, he's from Liberia. That's east of us. His body clock is like four hours ahead of us. Maybe they do things different over there," Mr. Grant said.

He took a puff from his cigar. "And don't forget, over there, *we'd* be odd."

"Don't matter. I've got a feeling that he's odd over there to," she said.

"Flora, will you cut it out? Whatever is bothering you, I'm sure it's nothing," Mr. Grant said, shrugging his shoulders.

Mr. Grant pointed to the kitchen. "Get another glass."

She walked into the kitchen and got the glass.

She handed it to him.

He looked at her. "Keep it. Sit down."

He poured the glass about half full. "Go ahead. This one is for *you*. Sounds to me like you can use it!"

Flora took a sip.

He stood up, got his evening paper from the living room sofa and went up to his room.

Chapter

Five

THE NEXT MORNING

Mr. Okimbi wondered when he would see the

woman: the woman, Marina, and with a gentle plant of his teeth

he could make his mark, the mark that would finally make her

his. He knew he could not see her in the morning. He could not

possibly go out into the morning sunlight. He knew he would melt

like an ice cube. He waited till it was evening so Mr. Grant could

introduce them. He wanted the 'approval' of the woman before

making her his.

He made an excuse to Mr. Grant the next day: 'a headache'.
Mr. Grant showed a slight disappointment.

"I'm sorry you're not feeling well," Mr. Grant said to him at the doorway of his room. "I've already told the Thomas' that you were coming and they really wanted to meet you," he said.

Mr. Grant shrugged his shoulders. "But maybe another time. I'll have Flora bring your breakfast and some aspirin up to your room, Sir."

"Thank you, Sir. Maybe tonight will be better," the man suggested.

Mr. Grant looked thoughtful.

"I've a few things to do today; some deliveries of my fruits and vegetables. Maybe that would be better. I'll call them, make your excuses and we'll discuss it when I return tonight," he said.

"That would be good," the man said.

Mr. Okimbi bowed gracefully from the waist and closed the door. Flora brought up his aspirin and breakfast on a tray and handed it to him at his door. Then, with Mr. Grant gone for the day, she ran as fast as she could for the stairs without saying a word.

Chapter

Six

THAT EVENING

HE GOT up at about five o'clock that evening. The

sun had began to set. He felt elated; rejuvenated; he was about

to meet Marina! After over a hundred and sixty years, he would

see her again. Marina! In his own warped mind, the years didn't

matter.

It would be dinner time soon and he put on a fresh dashiki robe.
It was clean, flowered and had been on hangers since his arrival the
previous day.

A t *close* to the dinner hour he heard noises
downstairs; *voices.* A few moments later there was a

knock at his door. It, again, was Flora and she backed away a bit

from him.

"Sir," she began, "if you are feeling up to it, Mr. Grant request the pleasure of your company downstairs."

The vampire Okimbi bowed and closed the door to his room. Without saying a word he followed Flora downstairs. She went into the kitchen and made herself busy there.

Mr. Grant looked at him as he came downstairs.

"Mr. Okimbi! How are you feeling, Sir?" he asked gayly, with a glass in his hand.

"Much better, Mr. Grant," the man answered.

"You couldn't go the mountian, so I've brought the mountian to you," Mr. Grant said.

***

There were two people standing next to him: one male, one female; *The Thomas'*; the female being the woman he had tread across an ocean to see!

Mr. Grant looked at him. "These are the Thomas'. After I made my rounds to all the stores I stopped by and asked if they'd like to come and meet you?"

Mr. Okimbi's eyes shinned. He could not take his eyes off of the woman, the beautiful woman, his long lost love from centuries gone by!; the woman he had traveled thousands of miles to see!

Mr. Okimbi was surprised by the cool response he received from Ann.

"...*Marina,*" was all he could say, but gently. *"Don't you know me?"*

"I'm sorry, what did you say, Sir?" Ann asked.

The vampire corrected himself.

"I meant to say, I do not mind this meeting at all," Mr. Okimbi answered.

"Good! Mr. Okimbi, let me introduce you. This is Doctor Stan Thomas, and this is his wife Ann," Mr. Grant said.

Mr. Grant turned to them. "Folks, this is Mr. Okambe Okimbi from Liberia and the person who's writing you've read."

"A pleasure to meet you, Mr. Okimbi," Stan said, extending his hand to him. "We've been waiting a long while to meet you, Sir."

"Yes, a pleasure, Sir," agreed Ann.

Mr. Okimbi shook Stan's hand. Ann shook his hand next. But he held onto Ann's hand a little longer; a little firmer. He was still surprised that Ann did not recognize him or even acknowledge him outside of Mr. Grant's introduction.

She looked back to Stan, her husband. And then she pulled her hand away from his.

Mr. Okimbi backed away from them both.

"A pleasure to meet you both," he said.

Mr. Grant looked at Mr. Okimbi.

"They're actually having dinner with us tonight, if that's alright with you?" he asked him.

Then he bowed to the both of them.

"It would be my pleasure to dine with the two of you. I apologize for not being able to come this morning," he said. "I was indisposed."

"Oh, that's okay, Sir," Stan said. "We understand. We don't mind meeting you half way: that is, going out of our way a little to meet someone so distinguished. We looked forward to this meeting. We've heard so much about you."

He looked at Ann. "Right, honey?"

"That's right, Mr. Okimbi! We've read your work on different cultures of the world. And we don't mind saying we were very intrigued by what we've read. Mr. Grant said you wanted to study us, or something like that. And we want to say, we don't mind if it will help your students and upcoming book!" Ann said.

"I am so delighted to have fans such as you," Mr. Okimbi said.

Mr. Grant extended his hands to the sofa and everyone sat down; Stan and Ann on the sofa and and Mr. Grant and Mr. Okimbi, on the smaller chair facing them. A coffee table separated the two men from the couple.

Flora brought in three cocktail glasses on a tray. Stan, Ann, and Mr. Okimbi each took one.

"Dinner will be up, shortly, everyone," she said.

And then she returned to the kitchen.

Mr. Grant had had a glass in his hands all along.

Ann took a sip from her glass and looked across the coffee table at Mr. Okimbi.

"So, how long are you going to be staying with us, Mr. Okimbi?" she went on to ask.

"Not much longer, unfortunately. As you know, my book is on civilizations of the world; how you eat; what you eat; how you act in certain situations. It won't take long to take a cab into town and to study you people, perhaps, talk to them. I have high hopes this book will establish me as one of the foremost authorities on modern civilizations of the world: to hear of their past, present and hopes for the future," Mr. Okimbi said.

"Fascinating, Mr. Okimbi!" she said. "I can't wait to read it!"

She looked at Stan. "Isn't that fascinating, honey?"

"Definately, most assuredly," he answered.

Mr. Grant interrupted.

"I'm sure his students back in Liberia will be very proud of him. He's a professor at Monrovia University," Mr. Grant said.

"Yes, you mentioned that," Ann said.

She took a sip of her drink and looked at Mr. Okimbi curiously. "Tell me, Sir, where have you been?"

"All parts of the world, Madam. My travels has taken me to Asia, Africa, South America, Canada and other places. And, of course, America," Mr. Okimbi said.

"That's a lot of traveling, Sir," Stan said.

"Yes. And one thing I have found already: People are people no matter where you go," he said.

"I feel your students are in for a treat. I hope we come through for you in the west. I hope your students will be greatly enriched by your findings here, and your readers as well," Stan said.

"I hope so," the man said, bowing.

From the kitchen Flora called:

"Dinner is served!"

She began placing bowls, napkins and plates on the next door dining room table.

Mr. Grant stood up.

"Well, you've all had Flora's cooking before. You know you're in for a treat!" he said.

Everyone stood up and went into the dining room. The vampire rushed and pulled out the chair for Ann and she sat. The men found a place at the table. It was a pleasant dinner; steak, rare; rice; green vegetables and more cocktail.

Ann, who had been fascinated with the African man from the very start looked across the table at him.

"It must be interesting, going from place to place, meeting all kinds of interesting people, writing about them: writing about their ways?" she asked, more of a statement.

"Yes; building them up; tearing them down. That is the bad side," Mr. Okimbi said, with a bit of humor.

Ann laughed a bit. Then she sipped her cocktail.

The vampire sipped his cocktail and looked across the table at her. He raised his glass slightly. "But none of my encounters are as charming as you, Madam. I could never say anything bad in that category."

"Thank you, Mr. Okimbi," she said, after a couple of seconds. "That's very nice."

"So when is this book coming out?" Stan asked.

"Very soon. I have several publishers interested," Mr. Okimbi said.

It was quiet. They continued to eat their dinner and sip their cocktails.

Mr. Okimbi looked at them. "I am more impressed wih you than you are with me."

"What do you mean, Mr. Okimbi?" Ann asked.

"Mind if I ask you a question?"

"Go ahead," Stan said.

"You live next to the Grant farm?"

"Yes," Stan answered.

"Why is it so called: *Jones Plantation* if your name is *Thomas?*" the man asked, directly.

"Oh, that's simple," Stan said, answering again and sipping his cocktail. "Ann's maiden name was *Jones;* her father was James Jones. She inherited the farm from him. Ann grew up there."

"I see. Nice inheritance," the vampire said.

The vampire paused. Then continued. "I understand both of you have thriving practices. Mr. Grant has informed me that you, my friend, are a well known General Practioner in these parts: and you, Mam, accomplished in your own right: a lawyer?"

"That is correct," Stan said.

"How do you keep up the pace? How do you find the time?" he asked.

"What pace is there to keep up with, Sir?" Ann asked.

"None. From the looks of you, and your attitude, I take it you like this. . . best of both worlds: this country living," the man said.

"Yes, we find noise in the city at work. But this is an escape," Stan said.

Ann continued.

"We like it," she said.

She looked at him curiously. "You've asked these questions, Mr. Okimbi; why do I get the strange impression that you already know the answers, despite what Mr. Grant has told you?"

"I do not mean to pry," he said.

"Oh, you didn't pry," Ann said. "You're here. We don't mind you being interested!"

Ann looked back at the man.

She took a sip of cocktail and almost chocked with excitement. "Mr. Okimbi! Wait! You didn't come over today, but why don't you stop by *tomorrow?* It would be a gas for you to see the place! You can see why we like this: as you say, 'country living'. Tomorrow, we are going into town on business; to do some work in our offices. Then, when we return, tomorrow night we're going to make a second trip; on pleasure; movie, theater; stuff like that. You are invited to both. You can come with us! You can see many Americans as they go about their way; interact with them; ask them questions and observe them *first hand.* It might give you a different perspective on your writings!"

"NO!" he said, sharply.

They looked at him a bit stunned at his quick turn down.

He looked around the room at all of them and sudddenly became as humble as he had erupted.

He retreated. "I meant to say: *'no thank you'*, for the visit tomorrow."

He turned slightly away. "I will be busy in my room writing and rewriting my paper. Also, I would like to read some of the many books Mr. Grant has provided for me. It will take up much of my day."

With his cocktail glass in his hand he stood up and walked into the living room. He folded back the curtains and looked outward into the night. "However. . . "

He continued staring outwards. Then he stared back at the others. "However. . . if I am still invited, I will gladly accompany you on your pleasure trip tomorrow night, if I may?"

He let the curtains go and walked back to the table where they were. He remained standing. "It may very well, as you say, give me another perspective on how you Americans live and act."

"Good," Stan said, elated. "We'll return from our business trip and pick you up at the house, if Mr. Grant will drive you over?"

"You're as good as there, Mr. Okimbi," Mr. Grant said.

"Excellent. I would love to see this place I've heard so much about," Mr. Okimbi said, under his breath.

He looked at Ann. ". . . And more of you, Madam."

Ann looked at Stan and backed away from the man a bit.

After a few seconds had passed she recovered and continued.

"Well, that settles it!" she said. "Mr. Okimbi, you're coming to see the Jones Plantation after all!"

They all stood and raised their glasses. Mr. Okimbi was last to raise his glass but eventually he did. Ann raised her glass a little higher than the others.

She looked around at the others. "To tomorrow night!"

"To tomorrow night!" Stan said.

Everyone took a sip of their glasses.

Mr. Okimbi sipped his glass and stared across the table at the beautiful Ann, his reason for being there in the first place; reuniting with her whom he thought was Marina his long lost love!

After dinner Mr. Grant accompanied the Thomas' out to the front yard. Mr. Grant and Stan was first to exit the house. Mr. Okimbi and Ann were last to leave.

Stan turned and looked at Mr. Grant. "Be sure to bring him by, Mr. Grant. We're just going into the offices but should be back no later than seven," he said.

"I'll make sure that he is there," Mr. Grant said.

Stan turned and looked at Mr. Okimbi.

"You'll see America in the dark, Sir, but you'll see it," he said to him.

"I look forward to it," Mr. Okimbi said.

They reached the center of the front yard and stopped.

Mr. Okimbi turned to Ann and then Stan. He bowed to them. "It has been a pleasure meeting both of you."

"The pleasure is ours, Sir," Stan said.

They shook hands.

He looked at Ann.

"And you, Madam, thank you for the conversation," he said, looking down at her. "It was most stimulating."

"You're quite welcome, Sir. And I look forward to seeing you tomorrow," she said.

She turned and headed for the truck. He went along ahead of her, opened the door to the truck for her and held it open as wide as he could, a feat that didn't go unnoticed by Stan and Mr. Grant.

She climbed in.

Mr. Grant looked back at Stan.

". . . Appears Ann has a fan," he said.

"Yeah; appears so," Stan said.

He looked at Mr. Grant. "Well, we'd better get going."

Stan joined Ann at the truck.

Mr. Grant came to the drivers side. He looked at Mr. Okimbi over the top of the cab.

"I'm going to drop them off at their house. I'll be right back," he said to him.

Stan threw up a hand at Mr. Okimbi.

"Good night, Sir. I'll see you tomorrow," he said to the Liberian man standing next to him.

"Good night, Sir," Ann said to him from inside of the cab.

Stan climbed into the truck next to her and Mr. Grant climbed into the drivers seat. The man only bowed and nodded his head.

Mr. Grant started up the truck and drove away.

As he was driving away he looked into his rear view mirror.

But the vampire was not there!

Mr. Grant looked over to Stan.

"Stan, I can't see him!" he said.

"See who?"

"Mr. Okimbi. He was there not two seconds ago but now he's gone!" Mr. Grant said.

Stan checked into his outside rearview mirror. But the image of the vampire could not be seen! Stan looked over is shoulder. But there was the man standing there, watching them as they drove away!

Stan looked over to Mr. Grant.

"Grant, look over your shoulder and tell me if you see what I'm seeing? Where is Mr. Okimbi?" Stan asked.

Mr. Grant took a quick look over his right shoulder and sure enough, Mr. Okimbi was standing there, just the way they had left him: yet, no trace of him in his mirror.

"What gives?" Mr. Grant asked, looking over at Stan.

Stan looked a bit dumbfounded.

He checked his outside rearview mirror. There was no trace of Mr. Okimbi.

"I don't know. Either he is a magician or we both need our eyes checked. What do you think?" Stan asked.

"I don't know either," Mr. Grant said. "He was there a minute ago and suddenly: poof!"

"Just keep driving. I'm sure that there must be some logical explanation for this. Somewhere," he said, as he looked at the road ahead of them.

Stan looked back into his outside rearview mirror. The image of the nosferatu was gone. Yet Stan looked back and saw them distancing from him!

Stan looked confused but said no more on the matter.

The vampire stood still, on the same spot; his teeth protruding below his bottom lips, his face turning green, but he himself, not moving.

He looked at the woman; the beautiful woman, Ann, and he reached outward towards her, his fingers long and wrinkled, his finger nails long and pointed.

Now that he had seen her, he wanted her more than ever!

Chapter

Seven

The Vampire felt satisfied. He had no reason to

be anxious; he had met the woman and had her in his confidence.

But now it was different! He knew their reuniting would be

different! He wanted her, but she had to be like him, a foul;

corrupt; a blood sucker; a leach; a creature of the night!

The next night Mr. Grant and Mr. Okimbi sat out

for the Jones Plantation. It was only about a mile down

the narrow road. It was still October and it was chilly. Mr. Okimbi wore a thick sweater underneath his Dashiki robe and Mr. Grant a

long coat.

Though the thought had crossed his mind, Mr. Grant said nothing of what he saw, or didn't see in his rearview mirror. He considered the Liberian man a 'guest' and didn't want to inconvience him with irrelevant questions.

He left the matter alone.

The ride to the Jones Plantation was brief, but it was long enough to get in more conversation.

The Liberian opened up with a rare conversation starter.

"Get's chilly in your part of the world," he said.

"Yes. It's winter time here. It can get down into the low twenties," Mr. Grant said, driving.

"Good."

Mr. Grant looked over at the man.

"I'm sorry, I didn't hear you," he said.

"Nothing. Nothing at all," the vampire said.

Mr. Grant kept driving.

The vampire looked over to him. "I hope they will enjoy my company."

"Oh, they'll enjoy you. They could *eat* a piece of you, Sir. I was talking to Stan after dinner yesterday and they're very excited about showing you around town; maybe getting an interesting tidbit or two on how you live, and of course, what you think of us?" Mr. Grant asked.

"I am sure I am more interested in you than you are of me. Why would I cross an ocean if it were not the case?" Mr. Okimbi asked, without looking at him.

"I'm sure you won't disappoint, Sir," Mr. Grant replied, still driving. "Just continue to tell them about yourself and from the looks of things, I know they'll be fascinated."

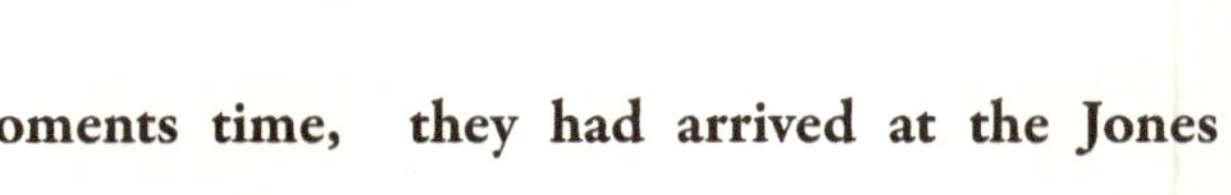

In a moments time, they had arrived at the Jones Plantation. Soon, they had come upon a large brick, two

story building that was the house passed down to Ann from her

father.

They could look beyond the house itself and saw wide open fields, land as far as the eye could see. There was, of course, a red barn nearby, with small hand tools leaning against it; a hoe, a rake and a shovel. There was a tractor parked on the outside; a typical plantation.

They climbed from the truck and walked towards the front door. The differences in their height was noticeable as the professor towered over the much shorter rancher, Mr. Grant.

Mr. Grant looked over to the vampire. "Think of this outing as being something excellent to tell your students when you get back."

"I will describe it to them in vivid detail," the man said.

Mr. Grant rang the doorbell. Stan answered the door with a wide smile on his face.

"Professor Okimbi! Mr. Grant! Come in! Come in!" he said, shaking the hand of Mr. Okimbi and then Mr. Grant.

The two men entered the front door and immediately sat on the couch.

Stan approached Mr. Grant.

He whispered: "Can I see you in the kitchen for a moment, Sir?"

"Sure, Stan," Mr. Grant said.

Mr. Grant looked at Mr. Okimbi. "Excuse us."

Mr. Grant followed Stan into the kitchen.

Mr. Grant looked at Stan. "What is it?"

"It's Mr. Okimbi."

"What about him?"

"It's his *hands*. They're as cold as ice! I noticed it yesterday at your house when I met him for the first time. It's like he shook hands with an ice pack then shook hands with me! What's with him? It's like shaking hands with a lead pipe!" Stan exclaimed.

"Is it that noticeable?" Mr. Grant asked.

"Worse. What's the temperature over there in Liberia? Maybe you meant: Siberia?" Stan asked.

"No, I meant Liberia. And their average temperature is not much different than ours," Mr. Grant said.

"And another thing; now that I think about it, why *didn't* we see him in our rear view mirrors as we were driving off last night? Did you ask him, Sir?" Stan asked.

"He'd gone into the house. It's the only thing I can think of," Mr. Grant answered.

"But we didn't see him! Yet there he was standing there - big as day!" Stan said.

"Maybe we were just imagining things?"

"At the same time?" Stan asked.

"I haven't the slightest: but I don't want to disturb our guest with trite questions on that subject," Mr. Grant said, reassuringly.

"Well, I thought you might want to know what I was thinking," Stan said.

"We'll keep it all under wraps," Mr. Grant said.

Stan looked at bit hesitant, but he complied.

"Okay. It's probably nothing. But I'll have to convince myself of that," Stan said.

"Try," Mr. Grant said.

Stan stood still. After a few seconds he grinned.

"Okay. I'll try. Maybe it was my imagination: the excitement of the day. I'll try to be more considerate in the future," Stan said.

He patted Stan on the shoulder.

"Good. Meanwhile, we've guest to entertain. Let's get out there before he thinks we've abandoned him," Mr. Grant suggested.

The two men returned to the living room. Mr. Grant returned to the couch. Stan put on his best behavior.

He looked excitedly at Mr. Okimbi.

"Sir, you want to see America at it's best; but at it's most vulnerable, right? Well, we have an idea. We've decided to take you to a place where you can see a lot of them at once! We've decided to take you to an amusement park!"

Mr. Grant looked at Stan.

"I think that's a fine idea," he said.

He turned to Mr. Okimbi. "What do you think, Mr. Okimbi? You'll see a lot of faces. How would you like to get out and stretch your legs a bit with nothing but fun: put away all your work?"

Mr. Okimbi looked at them both.

"The idea is very appealing," he said, lowly and dryly.

"Great!" Stan yelled. "I thought you might enjoy it with nothing to do but see us silly Americans all around you - acting silly!"

Ann came down a winding staircase located in back of the living room. Mr. Grant and Mr. Okimbi stood up.

She immediately extended her hands outward and went directly to Mr. Okimbi.

"Hello, Mr. Okimbi! Thank you for coming!" she said, excitedly.

He bowed and kissed her hand.

"Madam," he greeted her in his low, deep baritone.

He stood straight towering very high. "Thank you for having me. And if I may say so, that dress you are wearing is most *stunning!*"

"*This?* It's very ordinary, Sir," she said.

"It becomes you, Madam," he said.

"Thank you, Sir," she said.

She looked to Stan and back to him. "Did they tell you our plans?"

"They did. And I am very intrigued to see you Americans in this loose and natural way," he replied.

"Don't be too disappointed," she said. "Americans can get very odd at some of these places. But it's all in fun."

"We have theme parks in my part of the world. It is human nature to, as you say: 'let your hair down,'" he said.

"You do have a way with words, Mr. Okimbi," she said. Then she looked around at the others. "Are we all ready to go?"

Mr. Okimbi gestured to the door to Ann with his hand.

Ann took her coat from the rack near the front door and walked towards the exit. He leaned in front of her and opened the door for her.

She stopped. "Thank you, Mr. Okimbi. But I'm quite capable."

He looked into her eyes. She looked into his eyes.

He paused.

"You are, Madam. You are quite capable," he said.

His were *glaring; staring at her!* She tried, but she couldn't look away! She couldn't move her eyes away from his! She seemed motionless and *hypnotized* by him. *Captivated!* A prisoner in his gaze! She couldn't take her eyes away from him! They were fixated in his!

She didn't know it at the time but she was already under his spell! She felt faint but managed to sustain herself. She was trying to keep her balance. Then she looked back at him trying to help her; trying to help her remain upright.

Again she saw his eyes.

She had look of surprise in her eyes.

"Mr. Okimbi, you're staring," she said.

"Oh, I am sorry. I apologize. For a moment you appeared . . . unsteady."

"I'm fine now, Sir. I promise you, I'm okay," she said.

"Good. You do not know me very well. I can sometimes be . . . misinterpreted. I do not want to make you feel. . . *uncomfortable,*" he said.

Ann continued putting on her coat. Mr. Okimbi gentlemanly helped her with it on.

He gestured to the door again. "Shall we continue, Madam. Perhaps some fresh air, is in order?"

"Yes, that might do me some good," she said.

Stan greeted them outside and interrupted their conversation.

"What are you two talking about?" he asked.

"He was just telling me how much he's looking forward to this evening," she said.

She looked at him. "Weren't you, Mr. Okimbi?"

"I was," he said to her.

He looked to Ann again with the same peircing eyes. "She is very charming; and perceptive."

He looked at Stan. "I apologize for occupying her so."

"Well, whatever the case we'd better get on our way," Stan said.

Without saying another word she went her way to the car and climbed into the front seat. Mr. Okimbi watched with interest her every step as she walked away.

Stan looked at Mr. Okimbi. "She's just a little excited about seeing you this evening. She get's that way sometimes."

"Charming," the vampire said, bowing.

Mr. Okimbi walked over to the car with Stan and Mr. Grant. He climbed into the drivers side and bent down deep into his seat.

Stan went to the drivers side. He looked across at Mr. Grant.

"We'll drop him off later at your house," he said.

"Fine. I'll leave the front door unlocked for him," Mr. Grant said.

Stan climbed into the drivers seat and started up. He honked his horn.

Mr. Grant waved and they drove away.

In his bent position Stan could not see Mr. Okimbi from his rear view mirror.

"Mr. Okimbi, can you see our countryside from here?" Stan asked.

"To the contrary, I can see it fine from here," the man said.

Ann could only look back at her house, still with a slight headache. She rubbed her forehead again, wondering how she managed to draw a complete blank for a few short moments and wondered as to what could have caused it.

Chapter

Eight

It had been a quiet ride. Stan seemed content in

concentrating on his driving. When they reached the I-75

interstate that connected them to Atlanta. Stan looked into the

back seat at the man who was still bent over down in his seat behind

him.

Stan became curious as to his silence.

"Are you okay, Mr. Okimbi? You're awfully quiet?" he asked the
man.

"I'm afraid my reading and writing today has made me rather
tired. I guess I must have fallen asleep. But not too tired to not
enjoy your beautiful countryside. It reminds me of my own
countryside, beautiful trees and landscape," he said.

"That reminds me: what do you think of our place, Mr.
Okimbi?" Stan again asked the man.

"I think your place is lovely. It is an oasis," he said, in a low voice
barely audible. "The two of you look great together and are very

fortunate to have such a beautiful place and, of course, to have each other."

"That's very nice of you to say, Mr. Okimbi," Ann said, after a long silence. "Tell me, Sir, I understand that you are a bachelor?"

"Yes," the man said.

"Why haven't you been married? Isn't there someone?" she asked.

Stan looked at her.

"Ann, that's rather personal, don't you think?"

"It is okay," the man said.

The man looked away. He seemed genuinely thoughtful. "There was someone once, many years ago. She was young. We both were. She was beautiful, had soft skin, long hair and eyes that could light up a room. We were to be married."

He looked back at the road ahead. "But by unfortunately, it was dissolved."

"I'm sorry to hear that," she said.

"Don't be. Sometimes these things happen for a reason. Sometimes it reveals an even greater *opportunity* for one," Mr. Okimbi said.

"That's a good healthy attitude, Mr. Okimbi," Ann said.

He looked out of the window again.

"Yes. I have my work. I guess I am married to that. It keeps me traveling; meeting people. Young. Busy!" he said.

"We know how that is. It's not easy to maintain a farm and two careers at the same time," Ann said.

'Yes, you, Mr. Thomas, a doctor; and you Mrs. Thomas, a lawyer. I can understand how your situation must sometimes be. . . trying," he said.

"Yes, Sir. Sometimes it can be a hassle. But I wouldn't trade it," Stan said.

"And I don't blame you. My hat is off to both of you. You are both model citizens; a credit to your community. I will report that on my papers when I return, and it will be a very positive one," he said.

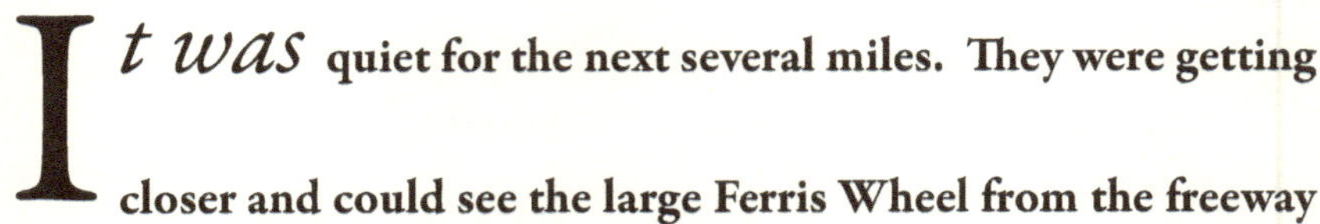

It *was* quiet for the next several miles. They were getting closer and could see the large Ferris Wheel from the freeway long before they had arrived.

At about eight o'clock they pulled into the *Peach Tree Theme Park* and it's parking lot where cars were being directed into stalls by officials with flash lights. They climbed from the BMW and eventually made their way to the entrance.

Mr. Okimbi reached into his pocket but Stan raised his hand.

"No need, Sir. You are a guest here. It's on me," he said.

"You are very generous," the man said.

Stan paid Mr. Okimbi's entrance fee and together all of them walked into the theme park.

People *were* suddenly all around them; in front of them and behind them. It was more people than Mr. Okimbi had seen at once since his arrival.

They began to walk, marveling at all of the bright lights that flickered or moved from left to right.

The 'bumper cars' were going, the 'spider web ride' twirling round and round, and carnival music was being played all over, although it was difficult to tell of it's source. As they walked no one seemed to pay much attention to the man despite his over six foot frame.

Ann looked over at him with a slight smile on her face.

"Lots of folks around, isn't it Mr. Okimbi?" she asked.

"Yes, there are," he said.

"Well, we promised you a crowd and I think we have delivered," she said, as they continued to walk.

They continued to soak up the sights as they moved along. The man's eyes wondered from place to place.

Ann and Stan were 'arm-in-arm'. After a few more steps she tucked on Stan's sleeve and whispered something into his ear. She pointed to a 'booth' a few feet to the side of them. Stan seemed to find humor at her suggestion.

She looked over at Mr. Okimbi. "Are you good at throwing a ball, Sir?"

"I beg your pardon, Madam?" he asked her.

She pointed to the booth to her right.

"A ball; over there," she said.

The sign over the booth read:

KNOCK OVER FIVE STACKS OF CANS
AND WIN!!!

"I have never tried such a thing," the man said, rather dry.

"Try," Ann said.

She led him over to the booth. She looked at the man standing there. "He'll take five balls, please."

The vampire (the man) awkwardly took the five balls, and with great strength and accuracy, he knocked over all five stacks of cans with five throws.

He surprised everyone. He won a stuffed animal. He handed it promptly to to the first child that passed by.

"Good throws, Mr. Okimbi," Stan said. "And a good gesture on your part."

"It was nothing. In my country, we threw balls playing in the streets. I suppose we are no different than anyone. Some of the areas are very poor. In many instances, it was all we had. Besides, courtesy is universal, is it not?" he asked.

"I suppose people are people no matter where you go," Stan said.

They moved on.

They arrived at a station that sold popcorn.

"Have you tried this crunchy stuff, Mr. Okimbi?" Ann asked him.

"What is it?" he asked.

"Popcorn," she said with some gayness.

"I have heard of this," he said, mildly.

She looked at the man behind the counter.

"Give him some," she told him.

Into a heated drum the man poured a scoop of hard corn and added butter. Within seconds the corn had popped into fluffy puffs and then he added salt. With a scooper he filled up a medium sized bucket of the puffed corn and handed it to Ann. She paid and handed the bucket to Mr. Okimbi. "Go ahead. Try it."

He did.

Ann looked at him. "How is it?"

". . . Good," he said.

Stan could only laugh.

"So now you are officially *Americanized,* Sir. You like one of our favorite carnival snacks!" he said. "Let's move on before she have you eat the entire snack bar!"

They continued to walk, taking in the sights, marveling at the large 'Spinning Wheel' and the 'Roller Coaster' ride.

Minutes later, Mr. Okimbi came forth with a rare abrupt statement.

". . . The chances people take for *amusement; for entertainment,*" he observed, under his breath.

"Yes, they do take chances," Ann said. "But it would be pretty dull if they didn't."

"Yes," he man said, simply.

About eight or ten teenagers came up to him.

"Hey, Mister? What kind of a shirt is that?!" a young girl asked.

He looked down at them, then at his shirt. He pulled out his shirt with his fingers. Then, as always, he took his time with his low key response.

". . . This?"

He looked back at them. "This is called a dashiki robe. I am from Liberia, East Africa. It is native dress where I come from."

"Can we do a selfie with you? And your shirt?" another one of them asked.

"What is that?" he asked.

"They want to take a picture with you, Mr. Okimbi," Ann stepped in and said.

"Go ahead, Mr. Okimbi; might be fun," Stan said.

The vampire was hesitant.

He raised his hand slightly.

"I am afraid that that would not be possible," he said.

"Don't be a stuff shirt, Mister," one of them said. "Come on! Let's get that shirt in a picture!"

They gathered around him quickly and the girl on the end quickly snapped the photo.

With the flash of the camera the vampire quickly knocked the camera to the ground. He dropped to his knees and let out a little scream. He cringed awkwardly and wiped his eyes.

"Ahhhh!" he cried.

He continued to cover his eyes. For a moment he was blinded.

Ann and Stan ran over to him.

"Mr. Okimbi! Mr. Okimbi! Are you alright?" Stan shouted.

They helped him to his feet.

The vampire collected himself. Then pushed everyone away from him. He looked around at everyone staring at him and he squinted his eyes.

He seemed apoligetic.

"I don't know what came over me. It must have been the light. It surprised me. I am okay now," he said.

He looked at the girls camera on the ground. He paniced. He raised his hand to it and shrieked away from it seemingly to put more distance between it and himself.

The girl picked up the camera from the ground.

"What's the matter with you, Mister? You weird or something? Why did you hit my phone?" she asked.

Again the man seemed humble.

". . . I apologize," the man said, standing to his full height, but from a distance.

Ann reached into her purse and handed the girl a twenty dollar bill.

"Look, you kids have your photo. Now please go away. Buy something. Okay?" she said.

The girl with the camera looked at the money.

"Gee thanks, lady! We just wanted a picture of that funny shirt!" she exclaimed.

The giggly teens walked away with their

photo and the image of Mr. Okimbi.

Stan looked at him.

"You sure you're alright, Sir?" he asked.

"Yes. I assure you, I am fine now. Shall we continue?" he suggested.

"By all means, Mr. Okimbi," Ann said.

Stan concluded:

"Sometimes those flashes can be very bright, especially at night," he said.

"Yes; so I have learned," he said.

They continued.

Soon thereafter, the young girl with the camera returned.

She looked up at Mr. Okimbi.

"Hey, Mister. I thought you might want to know, that picture we took, you aren't in it! You were right there on the end but your picture is *missing!* You're stranger than that shirt you're wearing!" she said.

She showed everyone the picture. Sure enough Mr. Okimbi's photo was missing and the rest of the teens showed up.

The teen girl kicked his leg and walked away.

Stan came over to him.

"Nevermind her, Sir. She's just a little animated. Americans get that way sometimes. Ignor it," he said, comforting him.

Stan looked directly at Mr. Okimbi. "Yet, I wonder why your picture didn't come out with the others, Mr. Okimbi? Any idea?"

"None. Very strange. And very puzzling," the man said.

"Yes. Puzzling," Stan said.

Stan thought for a minute. "Well, we'd best be on our way. How's your leg, Sir?'

"It is okay," the strange man said.

"Well there's a lot more park to see. Shall we continue?" Stan asked.

"By all means. By all means," the man answered as he was walking away.

They continued their tour of the theme park without further incident.

❧

S*oon,* after much gawking at more rides and faces and exchanging nods with strangers it had started to get very, very late.

They headed for the exit.

Before they sat out for the inbound trip Stan turned and looked into the back seat at Mr. Okimbi.

"We didn't mean to keep you out this long, Mr. Okimbi. You must be very tired," he said.

The man looked out into the night with an aire of excitement.

"To the contrary, Doctor Thomas," he said. "This is my *favorite* time of day."

Stan started the engine and soon they were headed back to the farm.

Stan reached over to get a cup of soda between Ann and himself. For the first time his vision happened to *align* himself perfectly with Mr. Okimbi who sat directly in back of him and the rear view mirror. Stan could not see him! Stan turned and took a brief look into the back seat while not taking his eyes off the road. There the man was, invisible in the mirror, but yet, very much in sight anytime Stan cared to look in back of him, something he had not noticed on the inbound trip!

Stan looked puzzled over at Ann who was quiet. It was the same thing both he and Mr. Grant he had seen the previous night at the Grant farm: no reflection of the Liberian in a mirror!

Stan no longer thought of him as the intelligent professor and brilliant writer whose papers he had learned to love so well. Instead, he began to question everything that had happened so far.

'Who was this man?' he asked himself. And 'Why was he ducking cameras? And with no reflection?'

Mr. Okimbi seemed oblivious to the discovery while staring out of the window in back of Stan.

Stan looked at the road ahead instead.

He didn't mention what he had seen to anyone. He still didn't know yet what to make of it.

They arrived at the Grant house about an hour later. A nervous Stan looked into the back seat.

"I hope you had a good time, talking to people?" Stan asked.

"Yes. I was able to see a part of America I cannot see from where I live or from books. It was most informative. Tomorrow, I will spend another day in my room; gathering materials, reading, and writing anecdotes of my experiences. It was most delightful and unusual. Thank you," he said.

"You're welcome. I think," Stan said.

Stan turned the rear view mirror towards the man. The man very quickly leaped from the car.

Stan jumped out after him. He grabbed Mr. Okimbi's arm.

He stared at him. "Who are you? What are you? I couldn't see you in the mirror. What gives?"

"Perhaps, your angle was wrong, my friend," Mr. Okimbi said.

Stan looked up at him.

"There is nothing wrong with my angle," Stan said, firmly. "Maybe it's you. Maybe it's you who's image wouldn't show up on that little girls camera; who's reflection wouldn't show up on neither Mr. Grant's rear view mirror or my outside mirror last night as we were driving away? Or just then, in the back seat. Maybe it's you?"

"Perhaps we are all just tired," the man said, staring at him with piercing eyes.

"Yeah," Stan said, staring him down. ". . . Perhaps."

Stan let Mr. Okimbi's arm go.

Ann yelled from her seat.

"What's going on out there?" came her loud voice.

He looked at her looking out at them.

"Nothing, honey. Nothing at all. We were just leaving," he said.

He climbed back into the car.

Ann looked at him.

"Aren't you going to invite him over. He's only going to be here for a week, you know?" she asked.

He looked at Ann who was still oblivious to his findings. From his seated position in the car he looked back at the man.

"Mr. Okimbi, Ann wants to hear more of your. . . adventures and she wants to invite you to dinner. Perhaps you can convince Mr. Grant to bring you by tomorrow?" Stan suggested.

Stan continued to look at the man with a strange stare.

Mr. Okimbi hesitated. But then he agreed.

"I think that would be lovely," Mr. Okimbi said, agreeably.

"Yes, Mr. Okimbi," Ann yelled from the passenger seat. "Please ask Mr. Grant to bring you by. He knows the time. We'll be expecting you. I may be a lawyer but I'm still a great cook!"

"I'm sure you are, Mrs. Thomas. And I will mention it to my host. I am sure it will be to his liking," he said, in a droll baritone way. "All things considered, I will see you both tomorrow night then."

He bowed.

"Yes," Stan said. "All things considered."

"Good night, Mr. Okimbi," Ann said.

Stan started up his engine.

The man bowed again. Stan's eyes never left him.

They drove away.

Stan stopped the car a little ways down the road. He looked over his shoulder and saw the strange man headed towards the front door. Then he looked into his rear view mirror and saw no man.

'It was strange,' Stan thought. 'Very strange indeed!'

Chapter

Nine

LATER THAT NIGHT

He appeared outside of the window of Ann and

Stan that same night. It was still pitch dark; the vampire would

have it no other way! He was clad in black, unlike his traditional

Dashiki robe. He had a black cape with a red lining. He seemed

to 'blend in' with the night. His ears were pointed! His face was a

greenish color!

Their room was on the second floor, facing towards a wooded area, thus making the house from that side mostly hidden from possible view. There was a twenty mile per hour breeze making the trees sway back and forth.

There was a slight drizzle.

He stared *hypnotically* up at her room. He whistled a slight tune.

Ann suddenly awakened from a sound sleep. She sat up suddenly in bed, her eyes *wide* and facing forward! She noticed the window was open and the night breeze blowing the curtains 'inward.' She went to the window with an attempt to close it. Stan was still fast asleep almost snoring. She looked downwards into the yard.

There, standing not more than twenty feet from the house was Mr. Okimbi!

Mr. Okimbi, true to his manners was creased; sharp; his posture still, his black cape flapping in the gentle night breeze. She let out a little shriek and backed away from the window.

He did not move.

Their eyes met. Though she seemed startled she seemed strangely *hypnotized* by his glare; arrested; and she could back away no further. His eyes became enlarged and she said 'yes' to his every silent command.

She turned and headed for the door, her arms almost straight to her sides and unmoving. She walked zombie-like down the flight of stairs, literally unblinking, through the living room and out into the front yard. She came to the yard where she had seen him as he directed her every step.

He gazed eagerly and defiantly into her eyes.

"Marina!" he exclaimed creepily. "Marina, my love. it *is* you! I can see it in your eyes; you still want me! You are mine, after all! There you are, my love, more beautiful than ever, Marina! Remember the good times we had! You are mine, and I will never let you go!"

He reached out and gently rubbed her face with the back of his green wrinkled hands and inch long fingernails. He stroked her hair. He stretched his arms wide. He pulled her closer to him and slowly he opened his mouth. His sinister upper teeth were showing. "Come now, my love, and be mine!"

He hid her from sight. She let out a little shriek. When she reappeared she had two bite marks on the side of neck; small but noticeable.

He released her and she walked back slowly into the house, up to her room and fell asleep in her bed.

***

Ann was up early the next morning. She was in the kitchen making breakfast before the sun was up at six thirty. She seemed to have more gayness than the day before, and she hummed a gay tune as she went about her way. She had no idea

of what she had been through.

"I'm going to work today," she said to Stan as he walked into the kitchen. "We are having a staff meeting."

"Oh?"

He sat in the dining room adjacent to the kitchen.

"Yes. I'm running late as it is. I have to be there at eight and it's almost seven thirty."

He took another sip from his coffee.

"Better get going," he said.

She sat bacon, eggs and toast in front of him.

He looked at her his eyes wide. "Gee thanks, honey. My favorite breakfast!"

He looked at her a bit closer. "Say, what's with you? You're up an hour early and you've made my favorite breakfast; what is it, my birthday?"

"Well, can't I make my favorite man his favorite breakfast once in a while?" she answered.

He stood up pulled her in close and kissed her firmly on her lips.

He pulled away a little.

"Thanks. You're amazing. I mean, here you are, late for work and you still find time to make a breakfast like this," he said.

"Don't get too used to it. I didn't have the time this morning. I just made the time," she said.

"Well, either way, you're a great girl," he said.

He kissed her quickly on the side of her face and motioned to sit down. He noticed some fluid on his hands.

It was blood!

He rubbed his sticky fingers together. He looked back at her. She had already started back towards the kitchen.

He stood up. "Wait a minute."

He walked over to her and made her face him. He looked at her neck. It was bleeding: slightly.

He lifted her chin with his fingers. "Ann, honey, you're bleeding."

She rubbed her neck and looked at her fingers.

She grinned a nervous grin.

"Well, seems I am," she said.

"Where did you get those marks on your neck?" he asked.

"What marks?" she asked.

He pulled her in for a closer look. He tilted her head to one side and touched them. "*Those* marks; the two tiny marks on your neck? Where did they come from?"

He took her into the living room where there was a full length mirror. He pulled down her collar and pointed them out:

". . . Those marks."

She was stunned.

". . . I didn't know they were there! I don't know where they came from and I've never seen them before. Maybe I hurt myself between last night and this morning," she said.

"Doing what? Sleeping? Did you fall out of bed or something?" he asked.

"I don't know!"

". . . Are you in pain?"

He examined her neck again. "It seems to be a bit volatile. Red. They weren't there last night."

"It's too small to be something. I'm sure it's nothing," she said.

"Honey, I'm the doctor here! Let me be the judge of that?" he asked.

"But It's *my* neck!" she replied.

Stan backed away.

"Okay. Okay," he said.

She seemed confused.

"I wish I had more of an answer. I don't know. I just don't," she said.

She rubbed her temples nervously.

He came a bit closer to her.

"Maybe you'd better stay home today," he said.

"Nonesense. We have that meeting remember?"

"Forget the meeting! I think you should go upstairs and go to bed until we figure out what this is!" he said.

"I'm going to work! Now relax, will you?"

She took off her apron revealing a sensible business suit. From the closet in the living room she grabbed a sharp pair of high heel pumps and put them on. He looked disgusted but he went back into the kitchen and sat back at the kitchen table.

"If you have any problems, call me here sat the house. I'm going to call you every hour, On the hour," he said. "I insist."

"You may do that, for all the good it will do," she said.

She came back into the kitchen and gave him an affectionate kiss on the top of his head. "Have a good day, honey."

She grabbed her briefcase and coat at the door and started out.

He stopped her at the door.

"But remember what I said," he yelled.

"I know, if it gives me any trouble, let you know," she said.

She blew him a kiss and rushed out the door.

Chapter

Ten

THAT SAME NIGHT

There was a knock on the front door at the Grant

plantation. The hour was very close to twelve. Mr. Grant had long

retired to his room. He couldn't understand who or what it could

be at that hour as he had already heard Mr. Okimbi return from the

carnival.

He came downstairs wearing a night cap and answered the front
door. There was a man standing there.

H*e was* of middle age and medium height and had

a little derby hat on his head. His coat collar was

turned 'up' as the night breeze was still a bit brisk. He looked to be

in his late forties or early fifties. He had on a dark suit, a dark tie

and was overall, by any standards, very well dressed; a briefcase

was dangling at the end of his right hand. As the door opened he

stood astute, flashed a smile and immediately took off his little

derby hat showing his salt and pepper hair, greying somewhat at

the temples.

Mr. Grant was scratching himself while looking at the stranger standing in his doorway.

"Yes? May I help you?" he asked.

The man sat his briefcase down and stuck out his hand to Mr. Grant.

"Mr. Grant?" he asked.

"Yes. I'm Horace Grant."

"My name is Jasper Wilkins," he said.

Mr. Grant immediately noticed the foreign British accent the man spoke.

"Glad to know you," Mr. Grant said, wearily.

They shook hands.

"I'm from England, Mr. Grant. I apologize for disturbing you at this late hour," he said, sounding even more British.

"I thought I detected a trace of an English accent. So you're English? What are you doing way out here? You lost?" Mr. Grant asked.

"That is what I hope you will let me explain, Mr. Grant. You see, I am *Doctor* Jasper Wilkins. I am a Ph D," he said.

"Oh, so you're a Ph D. Now what brings you all the way out here, Doctor?" Mr. Grant asked.

"I have traced your house here in America. I believe I can be of service to you; the people you know; and the people of this surrounding community," the man said.

"Oh? You can be of service to me? How? Why? What kind of a doctor are you, Sir?" Mr. Grant asked.

"I am a doctor of *paranormal.* I lecture extensively in the London area," he said.

Mr. Grant looked at him.

"Paranormal? Isn't that the study of things that goes *'bump in the night'*?" Mr. Grant asked, quite frankly.

"In a manner of speaking, yes, ol' chap," the man said.

"Is there much call for that type of thing, Sir?" Mr. Grant asked.

"In this case I'm afraid so. May I come in, Sir? It involves you and those you know. I think you will be most intrigued," the man said.

Mr. Grant looked the man over. He checked his watch. Other than the odd hour and his odd English dress, he seemed cordial enough.

Mr. Grant opened the door a little wider.

"Come on in," he said.

"Ablidged to you, Sir," the man said.

The man picked up his briefcase and signaled for a waiting taxi to leave. Mr. Grant gestured to the couch. The man sat. Mr. Grant sat in a smaller lazy boy easy chair facing him.

"Alright, Doctor Wilkins: talk. What's this all about?" he asked.

"I believe you have a guest here; a tall Liberian man that goes by the name of Okimbi?" Doctor Wilkins asked.

"Yes. He's sleeping upstairs. You have business with him?"

"My business is with you, Sir," Doctor Wilkins said.

"Oh? Explain."

"We may have a certain. . . situation on our hands; a delima; something of a very serious nature. Mr. Grant, what do you know about this man. . . ?"

He looked at Mr. Grant. ". . . I mean, other than what he's told you?"

"Nothing. He sent me a letter on his university stationary introducing himself. He said he was a professor in his country, Liberia, and wanted to come to America for a short while to study our ways. He said he did research papers on various cultures of the world and analyzed them for publication and presentation to his various classes. He wanted to include us: *American* culture in his studies. He showed proof that he has visited places like Egypt, Romania and even Britian doing his research. He wrote papers on his experiences in those places and sent them to me. I read some of his work - thesis papers, they were very fascinating. This guy has got to be one of the foremost authorities on world cultures. He said he was going to put his findings in a book. That did it for me. I invited him here for a few days to study us and our culture; our ways. It seemed like a harmless proposition, a renowned man of his stature staying here, don't you think? He does have a lot of references from colleague. They are exquisite. They speak very highly of him," Mr. Grant said.

"My good man, it is far from harmless. It's bloody dangerous," Doctor Wilkins said.

"I don't understand?"

He looked at Mr. Grant a bit closer.

"Did they send you his fake references, Sir? Did you fall for them? Apparently you have. Did they tell you that he was a university professor with credentials a mile long? Did they send you fake pictures of him that through his *influence* caused many to deceive you? Did they tell you that they were willing participants in falsifying his records, that the papers sent you were indeed written by someone else? That there is no book to be written; nothing of the sort," said Doctor Wilkins.

He looked at Mr. Grant and then at the upstairs in back of him. "And finally, did they tell you that he was an evil man; and that he has an evil and selfish purpose for being here?"

Mr. Grant stood up.

"Now see here, Mister. You're talking about my guest, Mr. Okimbi, a very important man!" Mr. Grant said.

"He is no guest. He is no writer. He is no instructor. By contrast, he is plotting and deceitful," Doctor wilkins insisted.

"What harm can he do: writing books?" Mr. Grant asked.

Doctor Wilkins stood up.

"Please sit down, Mr. Grant," he said, gesturing to the couch. "I have a strange story to tell you."

Mr. Grant slowly returned to his seat. Doctor Wilkins sat down also.

The man looked at Mr. Grant. "Sir, it would not surprise me if your 'guest' was not sleeping at all. It would not surprise me if he were not roaming about at night, prowling; like a wolf stalking prey."

"What in the world are you talking about?" Mr. Grant asked.

Doctor Wilkins stood up and began pace to the room.

"Yes, indeed, your Mr. Okimbi took a trip to Romania," he began.

"He mentioned that. So?" Mr. Grant asked.

"Did he mention that around the time of his trip there was an outbreak of *vampirism* there; hundreds of people coming down with a strange blood disease?" Doctor Wilkins said.

Mr. Grant looked amused.

"Blood disease? Vampirism? **Surely you jest, Sir," Mr. Grant said.**

"I'm afraid not, my good man," Doctor Wilkins said.

He came closer to Mr. Grant. "He did take a trip there, but not in the time you might think. The trip took place in the year *1890."*

". . . Eighteen ninety?"

The conversation stopped. Mr. Grant looked away.

He looked back to Doctor Wilkins. "That would make him over a hundred years old!"

"He's a hundred and sixty years old, my good man," Doctor Wilkins said.

"What? Impossible!" Mr. Grant said.

"Oh?"

Doctor Wilkins looked at him then looked away. He continued to pace. "When he returned from Romania to Liberia he was different; things were different around him. There was an outbreak of vampirism, people biting and being a part of an infestation; significant outbreaks of people complaining of blood loss; sleepwalking; wandering into the night. Coinsidence? I think not. I believe, through no fault of his own, he was bitten in Romania, the legendary *breeding* **ground of vampiric activity. I BELIEVE HE IS A VAMPIRE!"**

"No such thing!" Mr. Grant insisted.

Doctor Wilkins continued right through Mr. Grant's argument.

"There IS a such thing! He's a menace! He's traveling around the world, making the unsuspecting one of his kind! He's a creature! A creature of the night! A thing that walks in the night, preying on the blood of others," he said.

"That's the most ridiculous thing I have ever heard," Mr. Grant said.

"Doesn't it strike you as odd that he never goes out into the daylight, my good man?; that he only roams at night?" Doctor Wilkins asked.

"Why, I never payed much attention to it," Mr. Grant said.

"You should; you should pay much attention to it, Sir!" the man said.

"Well, even if it were true, why does it interest you? What is he doing here?" Mr. Grant asked.

Doctor Wilkins paused and looked back at him.

". . . He wants something."

"What?"

". . . He wants Mrs. Thomas," Doctor Wilkins said.

Mr. Grant's eyes widened.

"Ann? But why?" he asked.

Doctor Wilkins sat back into his chair and looked at Mr. Grant.

"Because he thinks it was she that loved him! He thinks *she* is the woman he once loved many many years ago; Marina Hollis. They were to be married. But for some reason she decided to marry someone else. He has never forgotten her. He has discovered her whereabouts here in America. In his warped, vampiric mind, he has convinced himself that Marina is Ann. And they are one and the same," Doctor Wilkins explained, in his English accent.

"That's preposterous," Mr. Grant said.

Doctor Wilkins took out a folder from his briefcase.

"I thought so to, at first. I traveled to Liberia, his home. There is now or never has been a Professor Okimbi," he said.

He showed him official documents of the current faculty of the university Mr. Okimbi claimed to be a part of. "There is no Professor Okimbi. There never has been. They were bitten somehow and came under his hypnotic *influence* when these documents were provided. He was able to persuade others to falsify records to deceive you. He is no teacher. He is no scholar. Don't you see? He is just an evil man that wants something; something he cannot have! Ann."

"How did Mr. Okimbi get to America?" Mr. Grant asked.

"I've studied this man's history. This Mr. Okimbi apparently was himself a man of means; a man who owned houses and property in Liberia. As I said, He visited America, on business, in the year 1890, met the beautiful Marina Hollis, fell in love but was jilted by her. Not only was he jilted, he was insulted," Doctor Wilkins said.

Doctor Wilkins sat on the couch. "A few years ago this Liberian man must have come across a likeness of Ann. And now he thinks he has rediscovered Marina, this woman he once loved back in America. He has returned here to reclaim her and to have her back," Doctor Wilkins said.

"After one hundred and fifty years? Is he out of hus mind?"

"No. He is just out of his element; crazed with affection," Doctor Wilkins said.

"I cannot believe that," Mr. Grant said.

Doctor Wilkins opened his briefcase.

"Believe it! But if you can't, then perhaps this will convince you, ol' boy. I've saved the best for *last*," the doctor said.

He took out a newspaper and showed him a small article on an American lawyer named Ann Thomas.

He handed the paper to Mr. Grant. "I told you he must have come across a likeness of Ann. I think I've found that likeness."

Mr. Grant looked at the photograph of Ann Thomas.

"It's an article on Ann," he said.

"Yes. And when I found out this Mr. Okimbi's travel plans, that's when I got suspicious. So I followed him here; almost to Ann's doorstep," Doctor Wilkins said.

Mr. Grant reared backwards on the sofa. He looked across the coffee table at Doctor Wilkins, the Englishman.

"But, Sir," he began with one last step at realism. "Even so, you and I know that there is no such thing as vampirism. The whole thing is ludicrous!"

"Is it now? I have traced his every movement, his every step in recent years. In every country he visited there were pockets of anemia; that is, blood loss. I'm convinced it is not a coinsidence. And I'm convinced now he wants Ann, to make her one of his own," said Doctor Wilkins.

"How so?" Mr. Grant asked.

Doctor Wilkins continued.

"Vampires need blood for their existance," Doctor Wilkins said.

He continued to pace the room. "No one knows how he became so infested. As I said, during one of his trips he was bittin, in some area of Romania by someone or *something* of a vampiric nature, a bat, a person. That is a theroy. Even so, he is a thing of the night now: and he knows that the only way he is to get her back is to make her one of his own: a foul and infested creature like he. That's where we come in: that's where I come in: we have to try and stop him," said Doctor Wilkins.

Mr. Grant became silent for a moment.

"Last night, the Thomas' were at my house. I introduced him to Mr. Okimbi. As I was driving them back to their farm we left him standing right in my front yard. But neither Stan or myself could see his reflection in our rear view mirrors. Yet he stood there in the front yard as big as day with the naked eye," Mr. Grant said.

Doctor Wilkins stood up.

He began to pace the room.

"A classic evidence of a vampire. Their reflections can never be shown in a mirror. It's like they didn't exist at all," Doctor Wilkins said.

Mr. Grant sat back on the sofa and rubbed his face.

He looked up at Doctor Wilkins.

"This is unbelievable. Positively unbelievable!" he said.

"We must stop him," Doctor Wilkins said, simply.

Doctor Wilkins looked surprised.

"How? If he's such a menace, how do you suppose we do that?" Mr. Grant asked.

"By our wits. And knowing a few of his weaknesses. It's all we have."

"I like those Thomas'. They're two of my favorite people. I wouldn't want anyhing to happen to them," Mr. Grant said.

He looked at Doctor Wilkins. "What do you suppose we do?"

"Be patient. Time is on our side. We know it takes *three* such bites on her neck to make her a full fledged vampire; a vampire like he is. I believe she has only been bittin once. We have two more tries to try to stop this evil," Doctor Wilkins said.

"You must have a plan," Mr. Grant said.

Doctor Wilkins walked away a bit. He looked back to Mr. Gtant still seated on the couch.

"I do. It is nearly daytime, he will be asleep. Like you, we must go to their farm and convince her husband, Stan, your neighbor to believe. The more of us against him, the better. We must act now! We must tell them of the delima they face; that we are up against a formidable foe; a form of evil, not before seen in this country, cloaked in the guise of niceness and good!" Doctor Wilkins said.

Chapter

Eleven

Ann and Stan had no idea of what was happening

right under their very noses; the delima; the mechanizations. To

them it was just another day of work for one, relaxation for the

other.

She was fixing breakfast over the stove when Stan came downstairs. Unlike when she worked, wearing a smart business suit, she was casually dressed in a blue turtle neck sweater and blue jeans.

She noticed Stan come into the room.

"Hi," she said.

He was fastening his shirt and tie.

"Good morning," he said.

He hoovered over the stove. "Ummm, uh! The smell of of bacon frying and coffee brewing always knocks me out of bed!"

He gave Ann a quick kiss on the side of her face.

He walked in to the living room, got his briefcase and brought it into the kitchen. He sat at the kitchen table. He took from his briefcase a sheet of paper. Suddenly there were papers all over the kitchen table.

She looked at him. "Patient list today?"

"Yep. I'm just going over it a bit to see if I can squeeze everybody in," he said.

He looked over at her. "And speaking of that, how is my number one patient today?"

"What are you talking about?" she asked.

"Those marks on your neck last night; are they any better this morning?"

"Will you forget those maks? They're no worse, they're no better!"

"I'm the doctor here and I'll be the judge of that," he said.

He stood up. "Let me see them."

He pulled down her collar on her sweater. His eyes stretched wide. "Honey, it's worse! Those marks looks like two large warts!"

He reached for the kitchen phone.

She yelled over to him.

"What are you doing?" she asked him.

"I'm calling Doc Prescot. He's a skin specialist, which is obviously what you need. I'm going to have him take a look at you," he said.

She came over and grabbed the phone away from him.

"No!" she screamed with some definiteness.

But she calmed down in a hurry. "I mean, I'm fine. So don't do that. I'm sure It's just a minor injury."

She gently hung up the phone on the wall. "It's not necessary, believe me. Give it some time and it will clear up by itself."

He looked at her with curious eyes.

". . . You sure?"

She looked at him a bit closer.

"I'm very sure," she said. "Now finish whatever you were doing eat your breakfast and get out of here."

He paused.

"Okay. But if they get any worse, I'm calling the doctor I don't care what you say," he said, sitting at the breakfast table.

"Okay," she said, much calmer.

She lowered the collar on her sweater. She brought over his breakfast and hers as well and she sat to the table next to him. "Better hurry or you'll be late. Isn't your first patient usually at 9:00."

He checked his watch gathered his papers and stuffed them into his briefcase.

"I'd better go. I'm late already," he said.

He stood up. "What are you doing today?"

"The office is closed today. A little yard work; feed the chickens, work in the garden. It'll be a full day," she said, not looking at him.

"Well, have fun," Stan said.

She stood up went into the living room and peeled back her collar. She looked at her wounds.

He looked at her. "You're concerned to aren't you."

She peeled down her collar and returned to the kitchen table.

"As I said, I'm sure it's nothing," she said.

She began putting the dishes away.

With his briefcase in hand he walked to the door, took his long overcoat from the rack and got his umbrella.

She turned and headed upstairs. She pulled down her collar as she climbed the stairs.

He yelled up to her.

"I'll see you this evening," he said.

"Have a good day," she answered back.

Again, she touched the two scars with her fingertips and for the first time, could not help noticing how evenly they dug into her flesh; how precise; how evenly swollen they were. She pulled her sweater collar up to hide them from view and hoped they would just go away. She sensed the scars were not ordinary, like a fall or an injury, but still didn't know what to make of it.

She looked pale and felt weak. She only wanted to go to sleep.

Chapter

Twelve

7:00 a.m.
STAN LEARNS THE TRUTH

Stan couldn't make it out the door. Mr. Grant

appeared at the front door, his hand in the 'knocking' position.

Stan looked startled.

"Mr. Grant!" he said, excitedly. "I was just about to leave for work. What brings you around so early, Sir?"

"I just wanted you to meet another one of my guest," Mr. Grant said.

"What?" Stan asked. "Another guest? What are you running over there Grant? A hotel?"

"No. It so happens it all happened at the same time," he said.

Doctor Wilkins stepped forward.

Mr. Grant looked in back of him. "I'd like for you to meet Doctor Jasper Wilkins. He's only going to be here for a day or two. He's from London, England. I thought before you began your day, the two of you should meet," he said.

"Well, now, Doctor Wilkins. It's always good to meet a fellow colleague," Stan said, smiling and extending his hand to him.

The two men shook hands friendlily.

Stan looked at him. "You're from England. What in the world are you doing all the way over here?"

"Yes," Doctor Wilkins began. "I am from London, on a holiday, Sir. I thought I'd see how you Americans behave for a while."

"Well, welcome to the States," Stan said.

"Thank you. Mr. Grant told me that you were a doctor yourself?" Doctor Wilkins asked.

"Guilty as charged," Stan said.

"As you say, it is a pleasure to meet a colleague," Doctor Wilkins said.

Stan invited them inside.

"Well now, come in, come on in, gentlemen," he said.

Both men followed Stan into the house. Stan sat his briefcase on the floor and put his coat and umbrella away.

He closed the door and gestured to the men. "Please sit down."

Mr. Grant and Doctor Wilkins sat on the couch. Stan came to the edge of the couch where they were sitting. "May I offer you gentlemen something to drink?"

"No thanks, Stan. It appears you were about to leave. I'm glad I caught you," Mr. Grant said.

"Oh?" Stan asked.

He sat in a chair facing them.

"Yes, you see, Doctor Wilkins is no ordinary doctor," Mr. Grant pointed out.

"Oh, Just what kind of a doctor are you, Sir?" Stan asked.

"I deal with the occult, my good man," he said.

Stan paused for a moment.

". . . The occult?" he asked, rather awkwardly.

Doctor Wilkins continued.

"Yes. In am a doctor of unusual things. My official title is a Doctor of Paranormal. I lecture extensively about such things in the London area. I teach others about things that are unexplained;

things we have no control of; things that are thrusted upon us that takes perhaps a third party to intervene," he said.

"And you are that third party?" Stan asked.

"Yes. I am," Doctor Wilkins said.

"You find this intervention necessary, Doctor?" Stan asked.

"I find it necessary at times," he said.

"Care to elaborate?" Stan asked.

"The intervention this time, Doctor, I'm afraid involves you, and your wife, Ann," Dr. Wilkins said.

Stan looked at the two men.

He stood up.

"What is this?" he asked.

Mr. Grant looked up at Stan.

"Please Sit, Stan. What Doctor Wilkins has to say is very important," he said.

Stan returned to his seat.

Mr. Grant looked at Doctor Wilkins. "Tell him, Sir."

Doctor Wilkins looked at Stan very straight.

"I believe the two of you are in danger; Doctor Thomas, especially her," Doctor Wilkins said to Stan.

"The dickens you say?" Stan asked.

Before Doctor Wilkins could say another word they heard a noise upstairs. They directed their attention in that direction. Ann was coming down the staircase. No one said a word as she ambled down the ten or so steps to the room. She looked paler than ever. She obviously tried to hide the redness of her neck that nearly came to her face, but her attempts were obvious and unsuccessful.

All the men stood up as she came to the back of the couch.

"I thought I heard noises," she said.

Stan took the initiative.

"Doctor Wilkins, I'd like for you to meet my wife, this is Ann, Ann, this is Doctor Wilkins, a friend of Mr. Grant. He's from England," he said.

"A doctor? From England? Well now, that is something. What are you doing all the way over here, Sir? That's a long ways to make a house call, isn't it?" she asked, extending her hand to him.

"As I was telling your husband, I'm on business, Mam," he said.

Doctor Wilkins and Ann shook hands.

"Well, it's very nice meeting you, Doctor," she said.

"A pleasure, Mam," Doctor Wilkins said.

Everyone took a seat. Ann sat next to her husband in a small chair facing the two men. The two men sat on the couch.

Ann was first to open up.

"So, what kind of a doctor are you, Doctor Wilkins?" she asked.

"Oh, a doctor of all sorts of things," he said.

"Concerning?" she asked.

"Concerning things that are unusual. Let's just say I'm a bit of a specialist," Doctor Wilkins said.

"I see. You specialize," she said.

"Yes."

". . . In what?"

Stan interrupted.

"Doctor Wilkins, my wife is a lawyer, being inquisitive is part of her profession. It gets in the way sometimes," Stan said.

"It's quite alright. I am a Doctor of Paranormal," he said.

Ann looked at him a bit odd.

". . . Of what?"

"A Doctor of Paranormal, honey," Stan said. "He investigates things that are unusual: things that go bump in the night, so he says."

She leaned backwards in her chair.

"Oh. I see. And you find that here?" she asked.

Stan looked at Doctor Wilkins.

"Apparently, he's going to try," he said.

Mr. Grant intervened.

"Ann, Doctor Wilkins lectures all oven the London area," he said.

"On that subject? Why?" she asked, innocently.

"When we find out we'll tell you, honey," Stan said, giving her a little kiss on the side of her face.

"Well, in any event, welcome to the States, Doctor Wilkins. I hope you find what you're looking for," she said. "Care for some refreshments?"

"No thank you, Mam. We didn't come to stay long," Doctor Wilkins said.

"Well, I hope you get your business taken care of, Doctor Wilkins, How long will you be staying?" she asked.

"Only a short while. Just a day or two," Doctor Wilkins said.

"That's not very long considering how far you've come," she commented.

"Hopefully I will get all my business done in that amount of time. I'm depending on it," he said.

"I apologize for being 'so inquisitive," she said. "I'm a lawyer and I guess it's just in me."

"Quite alright," he said.

Stan looked at her.

"He's staying with Mr. Grant, honey. He thought it would be a good idea for him to come over and meet us," Stan said.

"Well, that's very nice of you, Mr. Grant to think of us. The doctor here seems like a very fascinating person," Ann said.

She looked at Doctor Wilkins. "Well, again, welcome to the States, sir. And I hope you get your business done while you are here."

"I am sure I will, Mam," Doctor Wilkins said.

"Well, I'm tired. I just thought I'd come downstairs to see who's voices I heard. Good day, Doctor. Again, nice to meet you," she said.

She looked at Stan. "Honey."

She looked at Mr. Grant. "Mr. Grant."

She turned and headed up to her room.

Doctor Wilkins looked at her.

"Eh, just a moment."

Doctor Wilkins went to the front of her.

He examined her face and neck areas. "Mrs. Thomas, where did you get those marks?"

"Marks? I don't know what you mean," she said.

"Don't be trite; those marks that run vertically that you are so obviously trying to hide with this high sweater collar," he said.

He turned her head to one side.

She looked at Stan and back to him.

"They just appeared," she said.

"Nothing of the sort; nothing 'just appears' without cause; without reason, Mam," he said.

He looked at Stan. "Doctor, have you looked at her?"

"I have. She said she must have hurt herself; a slight fall," he said.

"Two scars; precisely the same look; a slight fall?" Doctor Wilkins asked, skeptical.

He looked at Ann again. "Forgive me if I seem intrusive, Mam. I'm just someone who is curious about something I deem, MEDICAL. If I were you, I would have those checked out. The scars are obvious and the redness is noticeable, even from a distance. And in my opinion, I don't think they're going to heal by themselves."

"Are you implying that these scars are somewhat an imprint of sort?" she asked.

"I might be. It needs further looking into, of course," Doctor Wilkins said.

"Believe me, Doctor, you're waisting your time with this diagnosos. It's nothing. It's just some sort of injury but they don't hurt. I'm fine," she insisted.

She looked at Stan. "Tell them I'm okay."

"She says she's okay," he said.

"Perhaps it looks worst than it is," Doctor Wilkins said, backing away.

Ann began to feel uncomfortable.

"Well, all this talk has given me a headache. I have a lot to do today. Good day gentlemen," she said, politely.

She started for the stairs.

She tripped and stumbled.

Doctor Wilkins was nearest to her and helped her to her feet.

She shook herself free.

"I'm fine," she said, and she continued up the stairs.

Doctor Wilkins came to the bottom of the steps and watched her climb up and reach the top. Stan came alongside him.

"I saw them earlier, those scars. What do you make of them?" he asked Doctor Wilkins.

Doctor Wilkins took another step away from him.

He had his back to Stan.

"An injury. Phooey. Nothing could be further from the truth, my good men!" he exclaimed.

Stan came alongside Doctor Wilkins for the second time.

He looked directly at him.

"Doctor Wilkins, you were about to tell me something back there. Now I'm willing to hear it," he said.

Doctor Wilkins looked at the seated Mr. Grant on the couch. Then he looked back at Stan.

"I think it is time for the facts, my good man," Doctor Wilkins said. "I only hope you are prepared for them."

"What is it?" Stan asked.

He escorted Stan back to the couch.

"Please be seated," Doctor Wilkins said.

Stan sat alongside Mr. Grant. Doctor Wilkins continued to stand.

He looked back at Stan. "I didn't want to say anything in front of your wife, but there is something that *must* be said."

"Okay. Out with it man!" Stan said.

Doctor Wilkins came over to him.

"I believe your wife is being stalked. Those marks on her neck are the clue," Doctor Wllkins said.

"Stalked?! By whom?" Stan asked, with a stunned look on his face.

"Doctor Thomas, I believe we are dealing with more that just a rash or an injury as you call it. On the contrary, it is the markings of something you have never heard of or imagined in your wildest dreams; in your wildest imagination!; something detestable! Something fiendish!" Doctor Wilkins said.

Doctor Wilkins remained standing and began to pace the room. "Doctor Thomas, you may scuff at it, but I have studied this genre for years. The markings are all the tell tale signs; two prick marks; a reddish rash around the neck, it could mean only one thing. . . "

He turned and looked at Stan. ". . . The markings of a *vampire!*"

Stan gave him a strange look.

Mr. Grant remained still.

Stan came to his feet.

He snickered a bit. He seemed amused.

"A what? Mister, do you know what you're saying? Do you know what you're implying?" Stan asked.

"I'm not implying it, my good fellow. I'm saying it outright. Your wife is being stalked by a vicious vampire that will stop at nothing to get at her. To bite her. I know what I'm saying, Sir. And the evidence is crystal clear," Doctor Wilkins said.

Stan looked at Mr. Grant sitting on the couch.

"Have you heard this? Is this what this is all about?" he asked.

Mr. Grant didn't have an immediate response. He only sat silently on the couch.

Stan looked back to Doctor Wilkins. "Isn't that supposed to be legend?; something out of a storybook?!"

Doctor Wilkins looked at Stan very straight.

"I beg to differ. You probably think that there is no such thing. But there IS a such thing and it exist, surprisingly, right in or own mist!" Doctor Wilkins insisted.

Mr. Grant looked at a confused Stan.

"Stan, Doctor Wilkins is an authority. He has studied this for years. He has come all the way from London, one of the spots where there has been infestations; people being bittin on their necks. Doctor Wilkins has traveled to many places and have studied these creatures and their movements. It has led him here!" Mr. Grant said.

"Well, what does he want? What's he doing here?" Stan asked.

Mr. Grant looked at Stan.

"Stan, I have investigated many cases, and what makes this case different is that, the vampire, through it all, is basically stalking ONE person: Ann. Your wife. He wants her! And you'd better get used to the idea!" Mr. Grant concluded.

Stan looked at Mr. Grant, then at Doctor Wilkins.

"You're both having hallucinations," Stan said.

He walked away a bit. Then turned and looked back at them. "What is this: *a joke?* Okay, why? Why does he: *it,* want her?"

Doctor Wilkins looked at him.

". . . To marry her," he said.

Stan looked at Doctor Wilkins then at Mr. Grant, one each at a time. "To marry her?"

". . . Yes," Doctor Wilkins said.

"But she's already married! To me!" Stan bellowed.

"A mere formality. He has no scruples. He thinks in his mind that Ann is the woman HE was to marry over a hundred and sixty years ago; and he has come here to claim her to make her a foul creature like he," Doctor Wilkins finalized. "It is the only way."

"Just for the sake of argument. . . Who's the vampire?" Stan asked.

Doctor Wilkins walked somewhat closer to Stan. He put one of his hands on Stan's shoulder.

". . . Mr. Okimbi," he said.

Stan looked away, then back at Doctor Wilkins.

"Okimbi? Why? What does he have to do with Ann?" he asked.

"He thinks she is the woman he was to marry nearly two centuries ago," the doctor said."

Doctor Wilkins took over the conversation. He began to pace the room. "Okimbi his been to America before, nearly two centuries ago. He was engaged to a beautiful American woman named Marina Hollis. But, unfortunately, she jilted him for another. He was left standing at the alter, so to speak, and he returned brokenhearted back to his native Liberia."

Stan looked away with a bit of wonder.

Doctor Wilkins continued. "Yes, Marina, rejected him for a man she knew before him."

Doctor Wilkins continued. "But something happed to Okimbi in the subsequent years. He traveled a lot; Romania, Egypt, London. And somehow, somewhere he contacted vampirism. In each case, the city where was showed an increased populous of anemia: blood loss, and an increased tendency towards vampirism, creatures that walk at night, preying off of others. Did Okimbi cause it? Perhaps. Likely. The tell tale signs are two bite marks around the lower neck, similar to the ones on Ann's."

He held up one of his hands. "But don't worry. Though I believe she has had contact with this man, it takes THREE such bites to make her a thing like him, a foul creature of the night! We have two more chances to right this wrong!"

"Why do you think it was him?" Stan asked.

"Romania about the time of his visit in 1890 was a source of vampiric activity. There was no trace of it before he arrived. We think, through no fault of his own, he was bitin and became infested there. Yes, your Mr. Okimbi is over a hundred and sixty years old! What happened to him could have happened to anyone. But it happened to him. I've studied the places this Mr. Okimbi visited and I'm sure of one thing: wherever he was, there was an outbreak of vampirism; across oceans; across European continents; across households. And here to, in America, if we allow it! You think he'll stop with Ann? She would only join him in his evil pursuits, to make others like them; perhaps follow him to Europe. She would only be his wife: a parter."

Stan sat on the couch. He looked dazed.

"How did he know to come here?" he asked the doctor without looking at him.

Doctor Wilkins continued. He paced some more. "After he was jilted, the man, this vampire, sought new faces and new romances, new conquests, but Ann was always on his mind. Yes, he traveled extensively to forget her. The years passed and ultimately he *accepted* he had lost her. But he came across a newspaper photo of Ann. He thought she was Marina and he has traced her here. In his warped mind, they are one and the same."

Stan stood up and began to pace the room.

"It's too fantastic! You could be mistaken about this. Maybe it's someone else you're seeking!" he yelled.

Doctor Wilkins walked over to the couch and sat on it. He opened his briefcase. He pulled from it the newspaper article on an

.

He put it on the coffee table.

"This is the newspaper photograph," he said simply.

Stan walked over to the coffee table and picked it up.

"It's a photo of Ann; a newspaper article," Stan said, quite simply.

Doctor Wilkins looked at Mr. Grant sitting on the couch.

"Wasn't that your reaction, Mr. Grant?" he asked him.

Mr. Grant only shook his head in agreement.

"Like I said, could Okimbi have seen this article and traced Ann here; thinking she was this Marina Hollis? I think so," Doctor Wilkins said.

Stan looked at him.

"It's a long shot but quite possible," he said.

"It's very possible. He knew what Marina looked like. We don't. We can only assume. Why would he appear here if there weren't certain similarties?" Doctor Wilkins asked.

Doctor Wilkins stood up. He put his hand on Stan's shoulder and walked away. "He is stalking her. Let's face it. Aparently, Ann must look something like this Marina Hollis he loved so. Why else would he be over here? Why would this mean so much to him?" Doctor Wilkins asked.

Stan took a moment to himself. He looked away and sat on the couch. He put his hands together as if in deep thought.

He looked at Mr. Grant sitting next to him.

"What do you think? Do you believe him?" he asked Mr. Grant.

"That's not the point. Do YOU believe him, my boy?" Mr. Grant asked Stan.

Stan looked away again.

For a moment he was silent. Then he spoke up.

"On that trip to the amusement park, kids tried to take his picture. His likeness wouldn't appear in the picture," Stan said.

"Vampires can never have their pictures taken!" Doctor Wilkins said.

Stan continued.

"And on the inbound trip, I noticed I couldn't see his image in the rear view mirror! As I drove around, in the mirror, he wasn't there!" Stan said, somewhat bewildered.

"And we couldn't see his reflection in the car mirror the night you met him," Mr. Grant added, referring to Stan.

Doctor Wilkins reiterated.

". . . AND neither can they be seen in a reflection. For all intended purposes, they are not even there!" Doctor Wilkins said.

Mr. Grant put a hand on Stan's shoulder.

"You said that there was something strange about him," he said.

"He was such a nice man, at first," Stan said.

"That is their camouflage. They are cloaked in the guise of niceness and good," the doctor said.

Stan looked away again.

He stood up and walked away with his back turned.

"Ann believes he's some kind of a saint," Stan said.

Doctor Wilkins walked across the room and stood in back of Stan.

"That is their way, my boy. The compliments. The bowing. Not that they're not sincere, but they always have ulterior motives. So believe what I tell you! His influence is very real. You must join me! Or we ultimately have no chance!" Doctor Wilkins said.

He stood up and looked around at Mr. Grant. "Not only is Ann in danger but imagine the many others who are at risk if he should succeed? The community. If he should succeed, the both of them will want more blood. They'll only be a team, creating other creatures like themselves. They will only widen their circle, till the point it will be overwhelming. For the good of Ann and the good of many, that may follow her, we must put a stop to this evil!"

Doctor Wilkins looked at Stan. "Are you with me, my boy?"

Stan walked even further away. He didn't answer immediately.

The room became silent.

Doctor Wilkins walked back to the couch, took the newspaper article containing Ann and put it back into his breifcase. Stan went to the kitchen wall phone.

Mr. Grant looked at him.

"What are you doing?" he asked.

"Calling the office and have another doctor to take over my patients. For the good of Ann, and the good of this community, I'm with you," he said.

Afterwards, Stan came back into the room.

Doctor Wilkins gave him a gentle pat on the shoulder. Stan looked at both men. "What happens now?"

"You follow my lead, my boy. Just follow my lead," Doctor Wilkins said.

Chapter

Thirteen

LATER THAT SAME EVENING

They didn't rush. They made coffee and discussed

how Doctor Wilkins in his travels had acquired records from

reliable Liberian sources indicating that there were some things

inconsistant to Mr. Okimbi's history. That, coupled with the fact

that there were no record of a Professor Okimbi who taught school

at a local university in Monrovia; that there were no classes being

conducted by him; no students; no record on what he did at

all and to the men brought his credibility down to *zero*. It only

indicated that he was indeed a man of means; records showing that about the turn of the century, Okambe Okimbi owned houses and

land in Liberia; also indicating that he had traveled to America:

met and had become engaged to a woman named Marina Hollis, in

America. But the actual marriage never took place.

They were all sitting at the kitchen table sipping their coffee.

"And this marriage won't take place either!" yelled Stan. "This will go no further! Not if I have a say in it!"

"Take it easy, boy. We're in this thing together," said Doctor Wilkins to him.

Stan looked away.

Mr. Grant sat his coffee cup on the kitchen table. He put a hand on Stan's shoulder. He stood up and walked away.

"This whole thing is MY fault. If I hadn't invited him here none of this wouldn't have happened. It's my fault for not having seen through his scheme right from the very beginning! 'A book writer': boy was I suckered," he said.

"It's not your fault. It's no one's fault. Records overseas are hard to come by. So much can happen in the *translation,* electronic or paper. Sometimes, you just have to take someone else' word for it. You didn't know what you were getting yourself into. So no one's at fault," Doctor Wilkins said.

Mr. Grant returned and sat quietly on the couch. He seemed to be avoiding Stan.

Stan stood up. Tall.

"Okay, Mr. Grant. *You're* forgiven. I agree this could have happened to anyone. But we're not going to just sit here and do nothing, are we?" he yelled.

From the kitchen table Doctor Wilkins looked up at him.

"We are doing something, Lad; we're being patient. It's our strategy," he said.

Doctor Wilkins took another sip of his coffee. With his coffee cup in hand he stood up from the table, walked into the living room and looked out into the yard. "This is a big house, but I think the three of us can guard it."

"Guard it? What do you mean, Sir?" asked Mr. Grant from the couch.

Doctor Wilkins turned to them.

"I mean, despite our disadvantage in number; we know he has the strength of six men; however, we have something he wants. We'll use her as bait," he said.

Stan's eyes widened.

"No. I refuse. I'll not put her purposefully in danger up against him. There must be another way!" he said, his chest stuck out.

"What else can we do? We'll be right here watching her: watching the house. He won't stand a chance with the three of us here - watching his every move," Doctor Wilkins said.

Doctor Wilkins continued to circle around the room. "So let him come to US. We'll lure him, right out in the open and this Mr. Okimbi of yours will have no excuses when we prove who we think he is!"

Doctor Wilkins had his back to them as he walked over to the open window in the living room. "As I mentioned to you earlier, It takes *three* such encounters to make a person like him; a foul creature of the night; a full fledged vampire. In my plan, we're not going to let that happen to Ann, or to anyone else. She has only been bittin once. He knows he has to return. And better still, WE know it."

Stan looked skeptical.

He looked at Mr. Grant sitting on the couch.

"Are you with this?" he asked him.

"I think the doctor is right. We'll lure him out into the open. We'll see him when he arrives. He'll have no excuses as to what he is. He'll know it: and we'll know it," Mr. Grant said.

Stan approached Doctor Wilkins at the window.

"And then what? What are we to use as weapons against this man? This thing? Our bare hands? Our smartness?" he asked.

He mimiced Doctor Wilkins. "Look, Okimbi, I know you have the strength of six men but I'm going to take you down with my smartness. . ."

Doctor Wilkins looked back at the two men again.

". . . these," he said.

He sat his coffee cup on the coffee table in front of Mr. Grant. He picked up his briefcase again and sat it on the coffee table. From it he took out three wooden sticks about five inches long and one inch thick. The edges had been sharpened.

Stan walked into the living room. Mr. Grant sat up straight on the couch upon seeing the wooden sticks.

He seemed curious.

"What are those?" he asked.

"One of the vampires few weakneses. And the one I think will be most useful to us all. He has the strength of six men, but a vampire can be destroyed by a single wooden stake through the heart; one plunge! He doesn't know we have these. He doesn't know we know of them. We'll surprise him. Each of you will carry a stake. Never let it leave you. It is your only defense," Doctor Wilkins said.

"Seems rather trite," Mr. Grant said.

"Trite but a fact. Let him come: with these, the advantage is ours. Without these, you'll be at his mercy! You wouldn't stand a chance!" Doctor Wilkins said.

They hesitated. They picked up a stick and examined it.

Doctor Wilkins looked at them. "You've been trusting me. You must continue to do so."

Stan and Mr. Grant looked at each other. Each man put a stick into his back pocket.

Doctor Wilkins looked at them. "Good. Now we're on equal footing with him."

Doctor Wilkins picked up his coffee cup from the coffee table. "He has come too far; too long a way, over a century to make finally Ann, or Marina, his 'bride'. He could have checked himself into a motel; and hid in the bushes and have gotten to her that way. But no: he made himself into a professor and let us wine and dine him, and we invited himself into our circles. And not only was he close to her, we allowed it. And now it is up to us to disallow it, and stop him from doing what he wants to do: making her a foul creature of the night as he is."

Doctor Wilkins picked up a stick and showed it to the men. "If we rush him, he can deny all claims to his evilness. But if we catch him in the act, well, that is quite a different story. When he comes, my good chaps, we'll be ready."

——— ❧ ———

It was in the middle of the day. Stan went upstairs to see Ann. Both Doctor Wilkins and Mr. Grant returned to the Grant farm to check on things there. The man continued to sleep upstairs, the place they knew he had made his 'lair'. They let him sleep. They dared not converge on him. They knew he was too powerful. It was a waiting game. They knew he would make his

move. It was only a matter of where, and when. They thought they

would be ready.

Meanwhile, they returned at the first sign of dusk to the Jones Plantation to surprise the ultimate thief in the very act.

Chapter

Fourteen

THAT NIGHT

Ann and Stan lay in their bed. The men, Mr. Grant

and Doctor Wilkins watched the front and side of the house. Mr.

Grant stood just below the bedroom. Doctor Wilkins watched the

front entrance.

At midnight, all was quiet. It was cold. Stan had loaned the two men two large overcoats. Mr. Grant was bundled up and rubbing his hands together as he came up to the front of the house where Doctor Wilkins was stationed.

"See anything?" Mr. Grant asked.

"Nothing. You?" Doctor Wilkins asked.

"Not a thing."

Mr. Grant looked at him. "Look, I'm going back to the house to check on him. It's too quiet."

Mr. Grant started off.

Doctor Wilkins yelled back to him.

"Grant! Take my advice and don't try to take him alone, Ol' Boy. I'd be suicide," he said.

"I won't. I just want to see what he's up to: from a distance, of course. I won't be gone long," Mr. Grant said, starting off.

Mr. Grant got to his truck, climbed in and hastened back to his farm.

⸺ ❧ ⸺

From his room, Mr. Okimbi saw his arrival and rushed back to his bed. Mr. Grant rushed from his truck and went upstairs.

Mr. Okimbi mimiced the sound of 'snoring' and made noises in his bedroom. Mr. Grant listened and knew that he was still there and half the night was gone! He was satisfied at hearing this and eased down the staircase to the first floor. He walked back to the truck. He managed to scratch his head. He expected more drama.

Meanwhile, his teeth showing, the vampire eased 'bat-like' down the back side of the house. Clad in his black suit that blended in with the darkness he began a rapid pace across an open field, almost gliding, towards the Jones Plantation. Mr. Grant started up his truck and headed in the same direction.

⸺ ❧ ⸺

Mr. Okimbi stood on the ground outside the Jones Plantation house in his black suit,   his prominent ears still pointed. He whistled once and Ann awakened.

She sat up with wide eyes in her bed. Stan was still asleep almost

snoring. She quietly put on her robe and walked down the stairs to

the front door and out.

Doctor Wilkins was laying face down, flat on the ground. He had been knocked unconscious by the vampire, Mr. Okimbi, who noticed Doctor Wilkins standing guard alone. She met him in the front yard, his fanged teeth still showing, his black cape still being tossed around by the wind. She walked over to him, his eyes wide with desire.

He stretched his arms wide, and she walked 'dream-like' into them, hiding her with his thick black cape. He turned her away so that no one could see the firm but gentle second bite he placed into her neck in the same area. He released her and she walked back to the front steps, past an outstretched Doctor Wilkins, into the house and up into her bedroom.

No one was the wiser.

Stan was still asleep as she climbed back into their bed. And she slept as if nothing had happened.

Chapter

Fifteen

At daylight Ann came downstairs. She was wearing a low collar revealing fully her neck and the redness surrounding it. For the first time she didn't seem to notice or even CARE that the scars were even there. *At the second encounter, she was unwillingly and unknowingly becoming more and more 'HIS'.*

She found Doctor Wilkins, Mr. Grant and Stan sitting in the living room. There was an atmosphere of gloom and she seemed startled at seeing them.

"Why, gentlemen, not that I'm complaining but weren't we doing this same thing yesterday?" she asked.

Doctor Wilkins had an ice pack over his head.

Ann noticed it. "Doctor Wilkins, what happened?"

"Oh, don't worry. I just slipped and fell: no big deal, my good lady," he said.

Doctor Wilkins put the ice pack aside. He stood up and walked over to Ann. He paused while staring deeply at her. "Mam, I must confess my concern. But there were footprints outside, they were neither Mr. Grant's, your husbands or my own. To be sure, these footprints were made by a man and a woman, of shall we say, unknown origin."

He came a bit closer to her. "Is there by any chance, one set of these prints were made by you?"

"Are you saying I'm sleepwalking, Sir?"

"I didn't say that," Doctor Wilkins said. "I'm only inquiring."

"Then how can they be mine? I've been in my room all night?" she said.

"Are you sure? Are you quite sure?" he asked.

"I'm positive!" she said, rather loudly.

She looked around at the others. "Say, what is this? An interrogation?"

Doctor Wilkins put his hands on her neck.

"The marks on your neck; they seem to have increased in size. They are more 'pronounced' than yesterday, and your neck seem noticeably REDDER," he said, with more determination.

He looked at her. "The sleepiness, the headaches, your scars, bigger than ever; it all makes sense! I think you had another encounter with him, the man we are after! What troubles me is where? And when?"

"What are you talking about? *Who* are you talking about?" she asked.

"It's my fault. It must have happened when I went to check on him. He must have seen me coming and *pretended* he was asleep. I thought he was asleep, and somehow, he beat me back here," Mr. Grant admitted.

He looked at Doctor Wilkins. "That was when he hit you on the head."

"What is everybody talking about?" Ann asked, almost yelling.

Stan stood up. He went over to her and put his arm around her shoulder.

"Stop it everybody!" he yelled.

He looked at Doctor Wilkins. "Sir, either you tell her or I will!"

"Tell me what?" she asked, frantically.

"Honey, you'd better sit down for this," he said.

He led her to the sofa and seated her next to Mr. Grant.

"And I'm inclined to agree, Doctor Thomas. I think we've gone far enough with this silence," Doctor Wilkins said.

He looked at Ann. "Mam, I think we owe you an apology."

"An apology? For what?"

"For leading you on when we all knew; you being the center of things," he said.

He began to pace the room. He looked back at her. "Those marks on your neck are not there by accident. They are not there by some fall or mishap as we have all allowed you to believe."

"Then what happened?" she asked, innocently.

"We believe you are beng pursued by something that is out of this world. Something foul and unruly. Madam, we believe you are being pestered by a vicious and powerful vampire! Yes, precisely what I said! A vampire!" Doctor Wilkins said.

Ann paused.

"You're putting me on, right?" she asked.

Stan looked at her.

"Ann, you are being pursued by this Mr. Okimbi. He is the vampire," Stan said.

"Now I know you're putting me on," she said.

Doctor Wilkins continued.

"Madam, his act is a facade that covers up the evil man that he is. He put those marks on your neck on purpose. And unfortunately, he was here last night. He has come here because he thinks he has found you," Doctor Wilkins said.

"Found me?"

"A woman named Marina Hollis, one he was engaged to marry her. But at the last minute he was jilted by her for someone else: a former beau. But aparently he has not accepted 'no' for an answer. And over a century later, he thinks he has rediscovered Marina! You! And judging from his track record, I believe there is no stopping him short of destroying him. He still wants you as his 'bride'! That's right, Mrs. Thomas, *he wants to marry you; because he thinks you are this Marina Hollis, that jilted him way back in the year 1890!*" Doctor Wilkins said.

"What? That's ridiculous!" she said.

"Mam, the records prove it. He came across your photo in a newspaper article published in England."

The doctor went to his briefcase on the coffee table and took out the newspaper article with Ann's picture.

He handed it to her.

She seemed shocked.

"That's me in this article!" she yelled with her hand over her mouth.

"Yes. Published overseas. Aparently this Okimbi man got ahold of this article which contained your approximate address in America. Remember, he had visited here before, where he fell in love with this Hollis woman. The two of you must look somewhat alike. In a crazy way, his warped mind has led him to believe that you are Marina! Mr. Okimbi believes it! And he is here to take you back! Mrs. Thomas, Mr. Okimbi is over a hundred and sixty years old!" Doctor Wilkins said.

Ann put her hand over her chest.

"That's ridiculous," she said, sitting down on the sofa.

"But it isn't! He is a vampire, Mam! A vampire! A blood sucker! Call it what you want! He has sucked the blood of hundreds to get to this point! Why should he stop now just short of his ultmate prize: you?"

She looked away and back to him. She handed the newspaper article back to him.

"Doctor Wilkins, I won't believe it! I won't stand for this nonsense!" she screamed.

She looked over at Stan. "Tell him it's nonsense!"

He touched her hand.

"It isn't. It's true," he said.

Doctor Wilkins approached her near the sofa.

"It is a fact, Mam," he said. "This Mr. Okimbi is not a good man. He is not here for a good reason. But I can understand. Over the centuries, a vampires main strength is that no one would believe in him."

Ann stood up.

"Doctor Wilkins, I'm loosing all respect for you. In fact, I've lost it! And I'll thank you if you would stop it! In the meantime, you will forgive me if I bid you all a good day!" she said firmly.

Doctor Wilkins looked at her.

He stood up and came closer to her.

"Please don't dispell me, Mam. You will be at his mercy," he said.

"Please leave," she said.

He approached her even closer.

"Madam, my good lady, you are a great lawyer. Your face is sometimes seen in places around the world. Yet, you balk at evidence right before your eyes!" Doctor Wikins pleaded to her.

"I've said my piece!" she said.

She turned away.

Stan came over to them. He took her aside and came in between them.

"Sir, I apologize for my wife's reaction. It's been very stressful for her lately," he said.

"I understand," Doctor Wilkins said.

He looked past Stan to Ann. The doctor took Ann aside. "May you have good day, Mam."

He went to the coffee table, picked up his briefcase and started for the door. Ann started upstairs.

Stan and Mr. Grant ran after him.

"You can't leave, Sir," Stan said.

He looked at Stan.

"I won't. I know what's at stake," he said.

He looked at Mr. Grant and back to Stan. "We will return to the Grant mansion. But we will return tonight. We, of course, won't try to subdue him. We will let him go and come here as intended. Neither of you will sleep tonight. We must all remain awake. With the three of us guarding and not leaving our post, there is no way for him to get through."

He reached into his back pocket and pulled out his stake. "And remember, you have your wooden stake. Tonight would be the THIRD bite. We cannot allow that to happen. . ."

❧

At the twelve o'clock midnight hour all was quiet.

From his bed at the Grant farm, Mr. Okimbi sat up suddenly his eyes wide and red. He was already dressed in his black formal wear that complimented him and that blended into the night. He stood up and began his one mile journey, through the same open field to the Thomas' ranch.

Stan was sitting in a folding chair below Ann and his second story window. He had on a thick coat and was chewing gum with intensity as he rubbed his arms to keep warm. He was also brandishing his wooden stake, occasionally looking up at the window where his wife slept.

There was thick brush behind him and he couldn't see him approach; the man walked through it without making a sound.

From behind, the vampire turned Stan towards him and picked him up by the throat with one hand. Stan attempted to stab him with his sharp wooden stake but he missed hitting the powerful man in the shoulder: drawing blood but missing the heart. The man tossed Stan ten feet into the air like a toy and he landed hard letting out a scream.

The vampire then showed his long canine teeth and began to move in on the half conscious Stan. But Stan took the chair and flung it at him. The vampire ducked but took the chair instead. He grabbed Stan by his arm and pounced the chair on Stan's head knocking him unconscious leaving him laying flat on the ground.

A voice came from the front of the house.

"Are you alright around there, Doctor Thomas? I say, Ol' Boy, are you okay?"

It was the voice of Doctor Wilkins, still guarding the front of the house.

But there was no answer.

Meanwhile, with his long crooked fingernails the vampire had crawled 'spider-like' up the side of the house to Ann's window.

When he came out, Ann was holding onto him 'piggy-back' style as he crawled creepily down the side of the house to the ground. Hand in hand, they began a hurried one mile journey through an open field to the Grant ranch house.

Doctor Wilkins came around the house to investigate.

He saw Stan laying on the ground, but coming to a sitting position. "Doctor Thomas! Stan, ol boy! What happened?!"

Doctor Wilkins knelt to him and helped him sit up straight.

Stan looked woozy.

Doctor Wilkins tapped him lightly on the side of his face. "Stan, ol boy, can you hear me?!"

Slowly and after several seconds had passed, Stan had collected himself.

He looked at Doctor Wilkins.

"He was here! *He was here!*" Stan yelled. "And you're right, he's very strong!"

Mr. Grant arrived from the other side of the house. Doctor Wilkins began to help Stan to his feet.

Mr. Grant came to the other side of Stan to pull him up fully.

"What happened?" he asked Stan.

Doctor Wilkins interrupted.

"He was here," he said. "But I don't know what happened to him."

Stan looked at Ann's window. The curtains were being taken 'in' by the wind.

"I closed those curtains and now they're open! Let's get to the room!" he yelled to the top of his voice.

They ran to the front of the house and into the front door. They hurried up the stairs to Ann's bedroom. Stan looked everywhere; even the closets.

She was gone!

Stan looked back at the two men. He rushed for the door. "He's got my wife! Let's go!"

They rushed down the stairs and into the front yard where they began a desperate search around the house.

Stan yelled: "ANN!"

But there was no answer.

Doctor Wilkins walked to the edge of an open corn field in back of the house. He knelt and examined the ground.

"Wait! More prints!" he yelled to the others.

The men rushed over.

Doctor Wilkins looked at them. "Two of them; side by side; one man and. . . one woman!"

He looked at the two men. "They've gone through the field! The Grant house! We must hurry!"

"The truck!" Mr. Grant said.

Stan searched the ground where he found his wooden stick. The men rushed for the truck and soon they were on their way back to the Grant farm.

———— ❧ ————

I*nside, the* vampire picked her up in his arms and started upstairs with her. The men burst through the front door.

"Ann!" yelled Stan, very loudly, as he entered the house.

Doctor Wilkins pointed to the bottom of the stairs where they were.

"There they are!"

With Ann in his arms he started upstairs.

The doctor yelled. "Stop, you!!"

Stan caught up with him at the top of the stairs and tried to wrestle him to the floor. Mr. Grant and Doctor Wilkins joined in the struggle to help bring him down. It did no good. The vampire's strength was too great and he managed to shake himself free of all three men. He dropped Ann to the floor. They chased him frantically down the upstairs hallway but then the hallway after ten feet came to an abrupt end.

The vampire's eyes were wide! He turned towards them.

He was cornered!

Mr. Grant drew his wooden stake.

"We've got him!" he said, in an offensive posture.

"He can't get outside, it's nearly daybreak!" Doctor Wilkins said.

Stan showed his wooden stake. He rolled up his sleeves.

"Let me have him," he said.

Doctor Wilkins showed his wooden stake.

"This is no time for selfish revenge, my good man. We'll take him together! Remember, aim for the middle of the chest; the heart, and push in deep! One of us may get lucky!" Doctor Wilkins said.

The vampire looked defiantly at them, his large pointed ears moving.

"Fools! You think you can take me?! ME?; who has transcended centuries?!"

He started to laugh. *"Ha! Ha! Ha! Ha!"*

Doctor Wilkins looked at the men.

"On my word!" he said.

He paused and prepared his stake. "NOW!!"

With their wooden stakes in hand, the three of them lunged at the vampire at the same time. The vampire pushed Stan to the floor. He grabbed Mr. Grant in one hand and Doctor Wilkins in the other and raised them high. With incredible strength he flung them backwards, Doctor Wilkins landing ten feet in front of him and Mr. Grant through the side rails, falling ten feet to the first floor injuring his leg. He was unable to walk.

With only two bites Ann seemed to be able to shake off the vampires oncoming influence. She saw Mr. Grant in his troubling position and rushed over to him.

"Mr. Grant!" she said, frantically. "Are you alright?!"

He seemed in pain.

"I think I sprained my ankle," he said to her, holding his foot.

The vampire then came next to Doctor Wilkins and Stan as both men lay groggily on the floor. He grabbed both men in their throats and flung them against the walls of the rooms, Doctor Wilkins hitting the floor hard and Stan hitting his head against the wall rendering him nearly unconscious.

Mr. Grant looked at Ann aiding him. "Go on upstairs! Go!"

The vampire saw her, but turned and ran into a nearby room. Doctor Wilkins was still on the floor rubbing his groggy head. He saw Stan in his inactive state. He crawled over to Stan and tapped the side of Stan's face slightly.

"Stan! Doctor Thomas, ol' boy! Are you okay?!" he yelled.

Ann came up the stairs and ran over to Stan.

She knelt down to him.

Doctor Wilkins yelled to her. "Look after him!"

She picked up Stan's head.

Doctor Wilkins slowly came to his feet.

———— ⟨҉⟩ ————

A *wobbly* Doctor Wilkins shook the door knob of the room the vampire had entered. It was locked. He picked up a wooden stake from the floor and placed it into his back

pocket. He took two steps backwards and with full force and his

shoulders he burst open the door.

———— ⟋⟍ ————

The vampire sat calmly and quietly facing him in a lounge chair in the *far corner* of the room. His legs were crossed; his long fingertips were together, and his face as greenish as ever.

"Come in, come in. Please close the door," he said, cordially, and smiling.

Doctor Wilkins gently closed the door behind him.

The vampire looked at him. "I suppose this is where it all ends, after so long a chase, so many thousands of miles? And I think, so much research you've put into this. But let me say, you are a formidable foe!"

Doctor Wilkins took a single step in his direction.

The vampire held up his hand. "Stop! No closer. I would consider that a threat!"

"Let her go! Forget this woman you are after! Go back under the evil rock you came from," the doctor said.

"I cannot. She is mine. She is my Marina," the vampire said, calmly.

"She is NOT Marina! You're confused. She is only someone that LOOKS like her! Let her go!" Doctor Wilkins said.

"You're interfering, Doctor Wilkins," the vampire said.

"I've given myself the right to interfer. I've made it my business to stop you. I've told you, you're got the wrong woman. What more do you need?" Doctor Wilkins asked.

"MY Marina. I need my Marina," he said.

"Marina is from another time: another place. What are you doing here?!"

"To take her back with me. To make her one of my kind," the vampire said, gently.

"That will never happen," Doctor Wilkins said.

"Oh? Do you think you can stop me? A mere mortal? That is a big job, Sir, even if, so far you seem worthy of the task," the vampire noted.

"I am worthy. And I do plan to stop you, any way I can!" Doctor Wilkins said.

"I have created others like me all over the world. You are only one man. Are you quite sure you want to try me, Doctor? I have good reason to continue. She is mine. What reason do you have to continue with this?" the vampire asked.

"Because morally, no one owns another person: at least not like this. That's why when I found out who you were; when I read that newspaper, I decided to step in. I followed you here. And I knew when I left, I was going to try to end this rein of terror!" Doctor Wilkins said.

The vampire stood up and turned away. He began to walk around the room, his hands behind his back.

"You call it a rein of terror, I say it is a soft heart. I've traveled many thousands of miles and over many continents to forget her. You must understand she is only one woman; but she is the one for me! I've had many wives, but she is special: beautiful, and together we can infest and influence many thousands of others to join us," the said.

He turned and looked at Doctor Wilkins. "Yes. I studied that newspaper when I saw her picture. And I knew I had found her. After many years I had found her and I had another chance to make her mine. I met her when I was like you: mortal. Weak. In love. But when I became like I am, I saw the opportunity to have her back. There she was: Marina! Finally, I knew where she lived: worked. It was all layed out for me. I made up the story, sent it to Mr. Grant, and he bought it. It was only left for me to come here, where we met, to claim her again; to make her mine again: my Marina!"

"But she is not your Marina! She belongs to someone else! Can't you get that though your head?" Doctor Wilkins asked.

The vampire paced the room some more.

"When these powers were thrusted upon me I went on a wild rampage. I must have infested hundreds. But through it all, I saw no reason to forget her. She has been on my mind. When I saw her again in that photo, I knew I had to have her again! I knew I had to go after her again!" he said, with some force.

Doctor Wilkins took another step in the vampires direction.

"I sympathize with you. And I'm trying to understand you. I know it's not your fault you were bittin in Romania and became a foul thing of the night. But it is your fault for dragging this innocent woman into it! I can't stand by and let that happen! She's innocent! This is all wrong!" Doctor Wilkins said.

"According to who?"

". . . Me!" the doctor finalized.

"And you still think you can stop me?!" the vampire yelled, his face turning green. "You still think you have a right to try; with my great strength?"

"I'm going to try," said Doctor Wilkins.

"For the last time, she is mine. Go while I let you," the vampire concluded.

"Don't let me. For the sake of her and the sake of others, I must destroy you," Doctor Wilkins said, swiftly.

Doctor Wilkins pulled from his back pocket his wooden stake.

The vampire calmly looked at the wooden stake. His face softened for the first time.

". . . A wooden stake through the heart of a vampire; a way to destroy him."

He looked at Doctor Wilkins in a disappointed way. "How primitive; how positively presumptuous, my good doctor. Just when I thought you were worthy, you fall far short. Surely, Doctor Wilkins, you can do better than that?"

"I must do what I must do, with what I have," Doctor Wilkins said.

"Put it away. You'll not get close enough to use that," he said, in his low baritone voice.

The comparison was evident. The vampire even at a distance stood taller and more powerful than did the scholarly Doctor Wilkins. Doctor Wilkins held fast to his convictions, however.

He held the wooden stake higher.

"I think I will get close enough," he said.

The vampire walked away then turned to him again, his ears had grown larger than ever and more pointed.

"So be it, Doctor Wilkins. And after you, what? There will be no one. She will be mine, after all. She will be mine," the vampire said.

"Not if I can help it!"

"Prepare to defend that!!!" the vampire yelled.

The doctor swallowed nervously. Yet he looked defiant.

"I'm prepared!"

T*he vampire* lunged across the large room at him. They struggled one on one. The vampire knocked the stick from his hands. Suddenly, Doctor Wilkins was completely defenseless, the two of them looking at each other.

They locked arms again and struggled around the room, knocking over furniture and lamps, each trying to gain the upper hand. But the strength of the vampire was overwhelming and it soon began to gain ground in the struggle.

He placed his hand on Doctor Wilkins' throat and began to choke him. Doctor Wilkins was suddenly beginning to feel faint.

Doctor Wilkins knew he could not defeat him with his hands. The only way to do it, he reasoned, was with his mind. His grip on the vampire relaxed.

He played 'opossum'; as if the vampire had won, and went limp under his powerful grip. The vampire thought he had won. He loosened his grip and backed away. Then he grinned and revealed is long, sinister vampiric teeth, with his dog-like teeth hanging at both ends. Slowly, he leaned into his male customer, opening his mouth as he got closer. Doctor Wilkins threw him over and backed away. He saw the stick he had lost during the struggle, ran over and picked it up.

The vampire moved in on him again.

"I told you that will do you no good," he said.

"And neither is your being here! Give up! Go away! You're on the wrong path!"

"Marina is mine!"

The vampire lunged for him again. Doctor Wilkins ducked away again and ended up several feet away at the window.

Over his right shoulder he could see the morning sunshine beginning to peep over the horizon. He noticed he was standing on a placement rug that extended from his feet to the feet of the vampire himself.

Doctor Wilkins looked at him.

"Well, what are you waiting for? Come and get me!" he said.

The vampire did. But again, he was able to elude his grip, using his shorter stature by ducking under him.

The vampire's back was suddenly at the window and it was Doctor Wilkins who stood at the *doorway* side of the rug.

"I won't miss this time," the vampire said, with sinister confidence.

The vampire started for him again.

It was his last chance. Doctor Wilkins dropped quickly to his knees and pulled the rug from under the vampires feet sending him crashing awkwardly backwards out the window and out into the bright morning sunshine.

Doctor Wilkins ran down the stairs past the others to the first floor.

"I need something!" he yelled.

He hurried into the kitchen and got two large shiny knives. He ran to the front door. The vampire was on all fours, crawling with much effort towards the front door and shade. The sunshine was getting through but was not strong enough to fully subdue him.

Just before and a few feet before he had reached the front entrance and shade Doctor Wilkins crossed the two knives in the sign of the crucifix; the sign of good. The vampire hollowed and backed away. He raised his hands and covered his face in an attempt to shield his eyes. It did him no good. Doctor Wilkins came in closer and closer.

With the sun at his back and the sign at his front the vampire had nowhere to go. Doctor Wilkins moved in even closer and with the sun getting higher and higher the vampire grew weaker and weaker.

Soon, and in a single plop, the vampire dropped to his belly, his long crooked arms still reaching out for more precious shade in the doorway just a few feet away.

"Please," he said, with outstretched arms and bloodshot eyes, looking up at Doctor Wilkins. "I only wanted to love her. . . "

But Doctor Wilkins continued to move in on him and soon, the sun caused the vampire to disintegrate right before Doctor Wilkins' eyes. And soon thereafter, the vampire was nothing; nothing but a pile of sand, a pile of wispy flakes, his long arms and fingers still outstretched in that position, a mere two inches from shade.

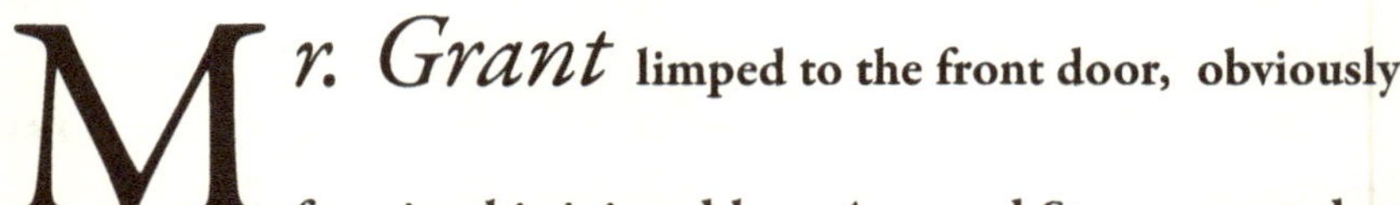

M*r. Grant* limped to the front door, obviously favoring his injured leg. Ann and Stan appeared at the front door behind him. She was supporting Stan as he struggled to stand. They saw the vampire finish crumbling. After

several seconds, Ann could not stand it any longer; she turned

away and put her face firmly into Stan's chest.

Flora, the housekeeper, arrived in back of everyone. She made her way near the front and looked at what was left of Mr. Okimbi.

She shook her head but retreated a little.

"Uh, uh, uh. I *knew* it I just *knew* it!" she said.

Mr. Grant limped over and took the knives from Doctor Wilkins' hands. Doctor Wilkins turned and went back into the house.

Mr. Grant looked at the vampire.

"He deceived everyone. But in the end, he only deceived himself, thinking he could finally mend his broken heart. Thanks to Doctor Wilkins, he didn't succeed," he said.

He turned and went back into the house.

Little by little, the remains of the vampire was blown away and scattered by the wind.

-THE END -

D*ear reader,*
Thank you for reading 'Blackula: the Vampire!' Won't you take a minute to post a brief, short, polite review? Honest reviews help readers decide if they would enjoy a book.

Again, thank you for the read and please have a nice day!
Sincerely,
-the author-

Don't miss out!

Visit the website below and you can sign up to receive emails whenever Walter Foster publishes a new book. There's no charge and no obligation.

https://books2read.com/r/B-A-BRFW-IFZDC

BOOKS 2 READ

Connecting independent readers to independent writers.

Did you love *Blackula the Vampire!*? Then you should read *The House on the Edge of Homerville*[1] by Walter Foster!

[2]

Frank Bonner is an escaped con on the run from the law. In Baltimore, Maryland he boards a bus to avoid being captured.

He ends up in a small town called 'Homerville' a little town he had never heard of. During a brief layover he meets and becomes friendly with a little old man at a local coffee shop. The little old man offers him $500 in cash if he can stay overnight - alone - in a local house that he himself owned on the edge of town.

DESPERATE for money Bonner takes the man up on the bet not knowing that it is a feat no one had done before and come out alive!

---

1. https://books2read.com/u/mgPLdR

2. https://books2read.com/u/mgPLdR

Also by Walter Foster

Tour of Atlantis
The House on the Edge of Homerville
Blackula the Vampire!
The Invisible Man
Blackenstein
Diamonds on Mars!
Fragments: Abort Martian Landing
Madam Black Soothsayer - Fortune Teller

About the Author

Walt Foster has always been a fan of mysteries and science fiction and he loves to write them. He is a graduate of Central Carolina Technical College in South Carolina. He lives in the United States U.S.A.

About the Publisher

The New Star Press - U.S.A.